LIBERTY PORTER,
First Daughter

New Girl in Town

KN

Read from the beginning!

ALSO BY JULIA DeVILLERS

LIBERTY PORTER, FIRST DAUGHTER

★ ★ ★ JULIA DeVILLERS ★ ★ ★
★ ILLUSTRATED BY PAIGE POOLER ★

LIBERTY PORTER,
First Daughter

New Girl in Town

ALADDIN
NEW YORK   LONDON   TORONTO   SYDNEY

ALADDIN

An imprint of Simon & Schuster Children's Publishing Division

1230 Avenue of the Americas, New York, NY 10020

First Aladdin paperback edition June 2011

Text copyright © 2010 by Julia DeVillers

Illustrations copyright © 2010 by Paige Pooler

All rights reserved, including the right of reproduction
in whole or in part in any form.

ALADDIN is a trademark of Simon & Schuster, Inc.,
and related logo is a registered trademark of Simon & Schuster, Inc.

Also available in an Aladdin hardcover edition.

For information about special discounts for bulk purchases,
please contact Simon & Schuster Special Sales at 1-866-506-1949 or business@simonandschuster.com.

The Simon & Schuster Speakers Bureau can bring authors to your live event.

For more information or to book an event contact the Simon & Schuster Speakers Bureau at 1-866-248-3049
or visit our website at www.simonspeakers.com.

Designed by Karin Paprocki

The text of this book was set in Bauer Bodoni.

The illustrations for this book were rendered digitally.

Manufactured in the United States of America 0811 OFF

2 4 6 8 10 9 7 5 3

The Library of Congress has cataloged the hardcover edition as follows:

DeVillers, Julia.

New girl in town / by Julia DeVillers ; illustrated by Paige Pooler. — 1st Aladdin hardcover ed.

p. cm. — (Liberty Porter, first daughter)

Summary: Nine-year-old Liberty Porter, daughter of the President of the United States,
starts at a new school and tries to be an exemplary first daughter.

ISBN 978-1-4169-9128-1 (hardcover : alk. paper)

[1. Presidents—Family—Fiction. 2. First day of school—Fiction. 3. Schools—Fiction.
4. White House (Washington, D.C.)—Fiction. 5. Washington (D.C.)—Fiction.]

I. Pooler, Paige, ill. II. Title.

PZ7.D4974Ne 2010 / [Fic]—dc22 / 2010000115

ISBN 978-1-4169-9129-8 (pbk)

ISBN 1-4424-0644-5 (eBook)

For Jack Hamilton DeVillers

LIBERTY PORTER,
First Daughter

New Girl in Town

Chapter 1

IF YOUR FATHER HAS BEEN PRESIDENT OF THE
United States for a whole week, there are a few
things you might want to know:

1. You shouldn't run through the first floor
   of the White House in pajamas. You might
   run into a press conference full of adults
   who will stare at you.

2. You should ask your parents *before* you
   decide that it's your mission to welcome

kids to the White House and invite a whole
tour group to play in your bedroom.

3. You don't automatically get a pony.

4. You do get a Secret Service agent who
   will let you talk to his friends over his
   walkie-talkie.

5. You don't want to eat too many of the
   White House chef's Porter Butter cookies.
   Especially the night before your first day
   of school.

Liberty Porter had only learned this last one this
morning. She had sneaked an extra cookie
after dinner last night. Okay, three.
And now she was lying in bed

with a sickish stomach. She was slightly nauseous and also slightly nervous. Because today was Liberty Porter's first day at her new school!

She had woken up way before her alarm clock was set to ring. It was so early that it was dark outside, but she couldn't go back to sleep. She thought about getting up and going out into the house. But she didn't want to wake her parents up. The president of the United States had to get a good night's sleep.

That's what her mom had told her the first morning, after Liberty woke up before her parents and went to the White House movie theater. She hadn't meant to turn the volume up *that* loud.

And what her mom had said the second morning, after Liberty had woken up before her parents and decided to play upstairs. She had planned to play the drums in the music room softly. But . . . well . . . they were drums.

★ ★ 3 ★ ★

So now she just lay quietly in her bed, thinking about the first day of school.

Liberty Porter was not the first kid who lived in the White House to go to school, of course. And some First Kids even went to school right *inside* the White House. President Lincoln's and President Hayes's children were homeschooled right down the hall from Liberty's bedroom. President Kennedy had made a first-grade classroom for his daughter and ten students upstairs on the third floor.

Liberty would go to a fourth-grade classroom at a nearby school. Everyone else had started at that school in the fall. Liberty would be the only new kid. And the only First Kid. Everyone knew she was starting school. It was big news. It was such big news it was even on the news.

"First Daughter Liberty Porter heads off for her

first day of school tomorrow!" the announcer had said on the television news yesterday.

Suddenly Liberty felt really, really nervous. She picked up her new beanie rottweiler, Alice.

"I've never been to a new school before," she told Alice.

Liberty did not know what this new school would be like at all!

Liberty had gone to the same school her whole entire life. She knew everybody. Everybody knew her. She had known that Perfect Paige would be perfect. She had known that Max Mellon would be annoying.

Liberty thought about her last day at her school. Most people in her class had said they'd miss her. They even made a card for her that said "We'll Miss You, Liberty!"

Liberty had felt sad when she'd gotten the card.

She even started to cry a little bit. She had sniffled and then blew her nose. Unfortunately she blew her nose a little loud and Max Mellon heard her.

"Ha!" Max had laughed. "Liberty snorted!"

The rest of the day Max had called her by a new nickname:

Pig-gerty Porter, First Snorter.

Liberty had a very cheerful thought about her new school: Max Mellon would not be there.

Then Liberty heard something outside in the hallway. Footsteps! "Franklin," she whispered. "Did you hear that?"

Franklin was sleeping in his dog bed in the corner. His ears perked up and he listened.

Who was walking down the hall? Liberty had an idea! Some people had said they heard footsteps in the middle of the night at the White House . . . and they thought it was Abraham Lincoln's ghost.

Seriously! People thought they heard or saw Lincoln's ghost. And not just any people, but presidents. Presidents Roosevelt, Truman, and Hoover all thought they heard the ghost knock on their bedroom doors.

Liberty had thought she wanted to meet Lincoln's ghost. But now she wasn't so sure.

And then there was a knock on Liberty's door! *Knock! Knock!*

And then the door opened. *Creeeaaaak!*

"Eeps!" Liberty squeaked. She dived under the covers. Her heart was beating like crazy.

"Liberty?" a voice said. Was it the ghost?

Her bedroom light clicked on. No. It was not the ghost of President Lincoln. It was just her father, President Porter!

Whhhhhew! Liberty's heart pounded a little bit slower.

★ ★ 7 ★ ★

"Good morning, Liberty Bell!" her dad said. He paused. "Liberty? Are you in there?"

Liberty crawled out from under the covers. She saw her father in the doorway. He was wearing his suit and tie already. Franklin got up and trotted over for his morning scratches.

"Hi, Daddy," she said.

"Happy First Day of School!" he said. "I know why you woke up so early. You couldn't wait for my Traditional First Day of School Porter Pancakes.

"You are one lucky girl," her father said. "It's your second time to get my traditional first day of school pancakes in *one year.*"

"Yup," Liberty agreed. "Lucky me."

"The best pancakes ever," her father said. "Nobody makes pancakes as good as mine."

Erm. Liberty didn't quite answer that one. Her father was going to be a great leader of the most powerful country in the world. But his pancakes tasted like soap.

"Just because I'm president doesn't mean I would give up making my famous pancakes," her dad was saying. "In fact, now we can call them Porter Presidential Pancakes!"

Liberty was hoping they could call the chef downstairs for breakfast. But the pancake tradition made her father so happy.

Maybe the chefs could sneak her something later. Liberty still couldn't believe she lived in a house that had chefs. They cooked in a huge kitchen downstairs. And not just a huge kitchen, but a pastry shop where they made cookies, cupcakes, brownies. . . . And not only a pastry shop, but a chocolate shop.

Yes, a whole room in her house where chefs made chocolate! Liberty zoned out for a minute thinking about the chocolate shop. *Mmmmm.* Chocolate shop.

Liberty jumped out of bed and followed her dad down to the kitchen. She sat at the table and watched him as he began to mix the pancake batter. He was wearing a long chef's apron over his suit so he wouldn't get dirty.

"What could be better than my special pancakes?" her dad was saying, peeking into the pancake maker. "Special pancakes for a special occasion."

Special occasion! Those two words made Liberty remember something. Something very, very good.

Liberty had been asking to visit the chocolate shop for treats.

"We need to save that for special occasions," her mother kept telling her. But now her dad said it was a special occasion!

"I need to go somewhere really quick," Liberty said.

"Be back in five minutes for your pancakes!" he said cheerfully.

"I will!" Liberty said, getting up from the kitchen table. She waved to Franklin to follow her out of the kitchen and into the hall.

Liberty and Franklin headed to the door that led away from the president's family's part of the house.

The White House has 132 rooms on three floors. The second and third floors are where the president and his family live. Liberty had gotten lost a lot the first couple days. But now she knew where everything was. Especially the most important places like the movie theater and bowling alley. And the chocolate shop.

Liberty opened the door to go downstairs.

SAM was standing right outside the door, ready to go. SAM was one of Liberty's Secret Service agents. SAM was very tall and had no hair. He always wore a dark secret agent suit and an earpiece in his ear and sometimes he wore very cool sunglasses.

"Good morning, Liberty," SAM said. "Good morning, Franklin."

SAM's job was pretty much to follow her around everywhere. Liberty liked him a lot. Franklin did too, because SAM had discovered exactly the right way to scritch him.

Franklin saw SAM and immediately plopped down on the ground and rolled over.

"Are you excited about your first day of school?" SAM asked Liberty, scritching Franklin's belly.

"Mostly," Liberty said. And then she looked around, and lowered her voice. "But first, we have a top secret mission."

"Proceed with instructions, Rottweiler," he said quietly.

Rottweiler was Liberty's Secret Code Name. Okay, her real official Secret Service Code Name was Ruffles. Ugh. So Liberty had created her own Secret

Service Code Name: Rottweiler. Much better.

"Follow me," Liberty said. She headed to the private elevator and pressed the button to take her downstairs.

"May I ask where we're going?" SAM asked her.

"Oh, just, you know. Downstairs," Liberty said as the elevator door opened.

"Hmm," SAM said. "Go ahead, Rottweiler. Go ahead, SCRAPS."

SCRAPS was Franklin's secret secret code name. Secret Canine Rover Assistant to the President. SCRAPS got into the elevator.

The elevator bumped down to the bottom level and Liberty skipped out and down the hallway.

Rottweiler had arrived at her secret location.

The chocolate shop.

Liberty closed her eyes and breathed in deep. Ah. Sweet, sweet smell of yum.

"Ahem," SAM said. "Before we step inside, do your parents know where you are?"

Liberty opened her eyes.

"Well," Liberty said. "You know how I've asked to come to the chocolate shop every day since we moved in last week?"

"Yes," SAM said. "Morning, noon, and night."

"Well, my mom said that I can only come here on special occasions," Liberty explained. "And my dad just said it himself. He said, 'Liberty! Today is a special occasion.'"

"Hmm," said SAM.

"Special occasion equals chocolate occasion," Liberty said. "But sorry, Franklin, you have to wait outside. Chocolate isn't safe for dogs. Poor you."

And Liberty walked into the chocolate shop. It was a small room with a long counter and lots of shelves. There was a chef wearing a tall white chef's

hat and mixing up a big pot of chocolate.

The wonderful heaven that was the chocolate shop.

"Good morning, Chocolate Chef of Awesome," Liberty said.

"And good morning to you, Miss Liberty." The chef turned to her. "Would you like to peek at today's creations?"

"Definitely!" Liberty said.

Liberty went over to the counter and saw a tray full of chocolates. There were chocolate-themed snowflakes and snowmen and snow women.

"Wow," Liberty breathed. "Just wow."

"Thank you," said the chef. "Today we have a winter theme at our lunch for honored guests. And now we also have an early honored guest. The First Daughter. What may we do for you?"

Well, Liberty had been thinking that the perfect *new* First Day of School tradition would be . . . chocolate for breakfast! She could have chocolate snowflakes, pan-cakes with chocolate syrup, and chocolate snowmen and snow women for dessert.

Liberty was just about to share her great idea with the chef when her cell phone rang.

Liberty looked down and her cell to see who was calling her.

POTUS (DADDY)

POTUS. That meant the President of the United States was calling.

Liberty loved her new shiny turquoise cell phone! Her dad had given it to her on Inauguration Day so he could stay connected to her. And usually that was a good thing. Except right now, when she was trying to get chocolate for breakfast.

"Hello, Mr. President," Liberty answered.

"First, pancakes are ready!" he said. "And second, I had this funny feeling you'd made your way downstairs. Perhaps to your favorite place in the house?"

Busted.

"Why, yes," Liberty confessed cheerfully. "I'm in the chocolate shop."

"Hmm," her father said.

"But Dad! Remember how Mom said I could only come here on special occasions? You just said that today was a special occasion!"

"That is a somewhat convincing argument," her father said. "What were you thinking of getting?"

Oh, great. Liberty knew chocolate for breakfast wasn't the best idea. And then she had a brilliant idea.

"Hot chocolate!" she said. "Cocoa for breakfast!"

Yummy. And something to wash down the taste of soapy pancakes.

Score! Liberty's father said yes, definitely, hot chocolate would be perfect with pancakes.

"Why don't you bring me a cup too," her dad said. "And—whoa!"

And . . . whoa?

"Whoa! I'm under attack!" Liberty's dad made a very weird noise.

"Dad? Is everything okay?" Liberty asked him.

"The sugar gliders are dive-bombing me!" he yelped. "They smelled the syrup."

Uh-oh! Liberty had two new pet sugar gliders. Sugar gliders are marsupials that have big blinky eyes and can glide through the air like flying squirrels.

She had named one Roosevelt, after President Roosevelt. The other one she had named Suzy. She had no reason except she liked the name Suzy.

They were cute. But they went a little crazy around sweet food. Like pancake syrup.

"Be right there," Liberty said into the phone.

"Rottweiler needs to be on the move immediately," she announced to SAM. "Mission: Rescue Rugged from Sugar Gliders."

Well, almost immediately. She waited until the chef put whipped cream and chocolate sprinkles on the hot chocolates. *Yum.*

Chapter 2

LIBERTY GOT OFF THE ELEVATOR QUICKLY. Well, not too quickly, because she didn't want to spill her hot chocolate with whipped cream and chocolate shaving sprinkles. SAM carried her dad's drink.

As they walked closer to the kitchen, Liberty and SAM heard her dad yelling, "Whoa! Yow!"

"Sounds dramatic," SAM said. "Smells dramatic too."

Liberty sniffed. It smelled like . . .

"Burnt pancakes," Liberty and SAM said at the same time.

"Maybe I should hold your hot chocolate while you save your father," SAM suggested. "Your drink needs to cool off, anyway."

"Wise idea, SAM," Liberty nodded. She looked around and lowered her voice. "Rottweiler is moving in."

Liberty slid down the hall in her slippery socks toward the kitchen.

One of her favorite White House people was standing outside the kitchen door. His name was Chief Usher Lee. The Chief Usher is in charge of making sure the White House runs smoothly.

Chief Usher Lee was cracking up.

"Are you laughing at my father?" Liberty asked him.

"No!" Chief Usher Lee said. "Well, yes. Yes, I am. I'm sorry but I just can't help it. See for yourself."

Liberty peeked into the kitchen and saw something funny. Very, very funny.

Roosevelt was clinging to the president's head! Suzy was attached to his ear. The president was dancing around and trying pull them off. But sugar gliders' fingers are very, very strong.

"Hee," Liberty giggled.

"Liberty!" Her father spotted her. "Help!"

"What happened?" Liberty asked him.

"I opened the syrup and they flew at me," he said. "I must have it in my hair."

Yes, it did look like Roosevelt was chewing on her father's hair.

Liberty moved closer and reached for the sugar glider.

"Roosevelt," she cooed.

Roosevelt flew-jumped over to Liberty. He dove right into his favorite place—her pajama pocket.

"Yay!" Liberty said. "Good boy, Roosevelt."

Then Liberty remembered that she had hidden a cookie in her pajama pocket the other night for emergency purposes. And that Roosevelt was probably enjoying a crumb right now.

SAM moved in quietly behind her father and *pluck!* He pulled Suzy off the president's head. Then he gave Suzy to Liberty to hold.

"Good teamwork!" her father said. "Whew!"

Liberty giggled. Her father's hair was sticking up from the syrup.

"I thought you would want to see the sugars before your first day of school, and Chief Usher Lee offered to bring them up," her father said. "It did not go as planned."

"Sorry, Daddy," Liberty said. She patted each sugar and they made happy noises.

"I think it's a good idea for Chief Usher Lee to take them back to their cage," Liberty's father said.

"It's past their bedtime anyway," Liberty agreed. Sugar Gliders are nocturnal, so they sleep all day instead of night. She said good-bye as Chief Usher Lee went to tuck them into bed.

"You look like you're ready to sleep all day too," her dad said.

Liberty looked down at her pajamas.

"I'll make more pancakes." Her father sighed. "You get dressed. Your mom is getting dressed too."

Liberty went into her bedroom.

So. She should get ready for school. Maybe first she would just take a slide down her bed. Yes! A slide! Liberty climbed up the ladder. She slid down the slide and into the beanie dogs that were piled up in the perfect spot for crash landings. Then Liberty jumped around a little bit. She practiced her headstand against the wall.

Then there was a knock on her door. It was her father, and he was carrying her hot chocolate.

"Liberty," he said. "I notice you're *still* in your pajamas. And upside down."

"Um," Liberty said, pointing her toes at the ceiling.

"Aren't you supposed to be getting ready for school?"

"Yes," Liberty said. "But I'm in the middle of a particularly excellent headstand."

Her father went and sat on her bed and waited. Liberty waited as long as she could, but the blood started to rush to her head. She sighed and kicked her feet back onto the ground. She rolled over next to her father and took a deep breath.

And a long slurp of hot chocolate.

"Okay, I'm nervous about school," Liberty confessed.

"I thought you were excited," her father said. "New school, new teacher, new friends."

Hello? That was serious pressure!

"I never went to school as a First Daughter before," Liberty told her father. "What if everyone stares at me?"

"That will probably happen," her father said, nodding.

"What if I raise my hand and answer a question wrong?" Liberty asked.

"That will probably happen," her father said.

"What if I trip in the cafeteria and I'm holding my lunch tray and I land face-first in a bowl of spaghetti? And someone takes a picture with their cell phone and posts it all over the Internet?"

Liberty flopped back on her bed.

"Goodness," her father said. "Well, if that happens, we will consider hiding out in the house until it blows over. I'd recommend the movie theater for our hideout."

Liberty laughed.

"However, there are no cell phones or pictures allowed in school, so you're safe," her father said. "I do have some advice for you, though. When you meet new people, don't bark. Don't bite. Don't jump on them with muddy paws."

"Dad!" Liberty said.

"Oops, that was my advice for Franklin." Her father smacked his hand against his forehead. "I was confused."

Liberty laughed. But then she frowned.

"You're very nervous, aren't you?" her dad asked.

Liberty nodded.

"I felt the same way last week on my first day," her dad said. "I'd never gone to work as a president of the United States before. So I thought of my oath of office when I said 'I will do my job to the best of my ability.' So my first piece advice is to try your best."

"I will my try my best," Liberty pledged. "What's your second piece of advice?"

"Change out of your pajamas," her father said.

"Oh yeah!" Liberty said, looking down. "Remember when I wore pajamas to that press conference?

Ack! That was probably the Most Embarrassing Clothes Moment in White House history."

"Not quite," her father smiled. "President John Quincy Adams liked to swim naked in the Potomac river. Once a reporter followed him and hid his clothes while he was swimming. She wouldn't give them back until he gave her an interview."

Hee hee hee. That *would* be more embarrassing.

Most Embarrassing
Clothes Moment in
WHITE HOUSE
HISTORY

Chapter 3

IT WAS TIME FOR ANOTHER PORTER FAMILY FIRST Day of School Tradition. Every year, Liberty's father took a picture of her and Franklin on their front step. This year, they had a new front step.

And a new photographer. The White House had an official photographer, who took pictures of her father throughout the day.

Liberty came out of her room and went to her kitchen.

"I'm ready for my pictures!" Liberty smiled. "How do I look?"

Liberty stood up and twirled. Then she struck a supermodel pose. She walked the catwalk, which was really the hall near the kitchen.

Work it, Liberty! It's Liberty Porter, First Daughter, on the runway and super-stylish in her first-day-of-school outfit. Has there ever been a First Daughter so ready? So polished?

Liberty posed in front of her dad.

"You look wonderful," her dad said. "However, may I ask if the hot chocolate mustache is supposed to be part of your look?"

Liberty ran to the mirror in the hall. Oops. Chocolate was smeared across her top lip. Oh. So, she probably was not the most polished First Daughter.

"I can still take the traditional pictures if you want me to," her father had told her. "I can make my pancakes and I can take my pictures."

"It's okay," Liberty assured him. "We should

probably use the official photographer."

Liberty's father had many talents. Taking pictures was not one of them.

In kindergarten, her picture was blurry. In first grade, she was blinking. In second grade, it looked like she had half a head. In third grade, she was blurry again.

This year, she was hoping to be un-blurry and with a whole head.

Suddenly, Franklin growled. Then he ran to the door. Then he ran over to Liberty and around in circles, barking at her.

Erg. Franklin acting spazzy meant one thing: Miss Crum was coming. Miss Crum was the president's chief of staff. The chief of staff is in charge of the president's schedule. Liberty knew that part of her job was to be kind of bossy. But Miss Crum also liked to boss Liberty around. And even boss Franklin!

"Thanks for the heads-up," Liberty told him. She ran to the mirror and made sure she had no hot chocolate on her face. She patted her hair down a bit.

Liberty heard the *click click* of high heels coming her way. She pasted on a smile.

"Good morning, Ruffles!" Miss Crum said as she came in. "Don't you look precious today."

"Thank you, Miss Crum," Liberty said.

"Liberty," she said. "I thought you would like someone who knows the ropes to accompany you to school."

Erg. Erg. Miss Crum wanted to go to school with Liberty?

Then Franklin suddenly barked again. But this time his tail was wagging.

And James walked into the room! James was Liberty's newest friend. She met him when she moved into the White House. They were going to the same school. James would be in a different class, though.

"Hi, Liberty. Hope it's okay if I go with you to school," James said. "It was my mom's idea to surprise you. And since Miss Crum was coming in for work, she brought me."

Yes!

"Your mom's idea is great!" Liberty told him. *For once.* She didn't say that part out loud.

James leaned down and gave Franklin some pats on the head.

"I need to go over the day's schedule with your father, Liberty. James, why don't you share tips about your school?" Miss Crum said.

Miss Crum thought James would be a good influence on Liberty.

His mother was Mrs. Piffle, chief of protocol. Protocol meant manners. James had been taught lots of manners.

"Oh no, James!" Liberty said. "You're wearing your shoes! Take off your shoes!"

"Oh!" James said, taking off his shoes. "Sorry! I can't believe I wore shoes in the house. Did I get anything dirty?"

"That's not what I mean," Liberty said. "It's time for . . . superslide challenge!"

Liberty took a running start. And . . . *woooosh!* She slid down the hall. She was going at least two thousand miles an hour.

Woo-hoo!

James grinned. Liberty had taught him her spectacular sliding techniques.

"Come on, James!" she yelled.

James grinned and took a running start and . . . *woooosh!*

"You're getting faster!" Liberty complimented him.

They took a running start and *wooosh!* They slid down the hall together.

"Good gracious!" gasped Miss Crum as they zoomed past her down the hall.

"I wonder if we have time to slide down the Ramp of the Rump," Liberty called to James. That's what she called the ramp to a room called the Solarium. You could slide all the way down—on your butt!

"No ramps or rumps!" Miss Crum's voice called down the hall. "The photographer is almost ready for you."

Okay, fine.

"I better go say my good-byes," Liberty decided.

"Good-bye to who?" James asked. He followed

Liberty to her bedroom. Liberty went over to her collection of beanie dogs.

"Good-bye, Bradley," Liberty said, giving her black-and-white smiley dog a hug. Then she turned to her rottweiler. "Goodbye, Alice."

"Liberty, you have thirty-seven beanie dogs," James said. "I don't think you'll have time for good-byes to every one."

"You're right," Liberty said. "I don't want anyone to feel left out. Good-bye beanie dogs! Good-bye dolls and miniature ponies! Good-bye Bonus Brothers!"

"You talk to your posters?" James asked her.

"Um, maybe," Liberty admitted. "And now we have one more good-bye. We have to say good-bye to President Lincoln's ghost!"

"Uh, maybe I'll wait over here," James said.

James was a little spooked by the idea of the ghost.

"President Lincoln, I have to go to school! I just

wanted to say bye!" Liberty called out. Then she went back to James.

"Did you know that Lincoln did most of his school at home?" James said. "And when he did go to school he had to walk two miles to get to a one-room log cabin? Even through the snow?"

Brr!

"And most of his education was from reading books by himself," James said. "He loved books so much he once walked twenty miles to borrow a book."

"We're seriously lucky we have our libraries and bookstores," Liberty said.

"Agreed," James nodded.

"Did somebody say two of my favorite words: libraries and bookstores?" Liberty's mom came around the corner. "Of course, along with 'daughter,' 'husband,' and 'pets.'

Liberty's mom loved books so much her Secret

Service Code Name was Reader. It fit her way better than Ruffles fit Liberty!

"Speaking of books, here is your book bag," her mom said. "And your coat and scarf for your pictures. The photographer is going to take them outside in the gardens."

Liberty and James followed the First Lady out to the gardens.

There were a couple of gardens around the White House that had famous colorful flowers. But not so much right now, because it was winter.

The most famous one was the Rose Garden, which was outside her dad's window in the Oval Office.

There also was the First Lady's Garden that grew roses and pretty blue flowers called salvias and had lots of bees.

There was a fairly new White House vegetable garden. The first president who lived in the White

House was John Adams. He planted the first White House vegetable garden. Liberty's mom had told her that the gardens grew most of the food for the first presidents who lived there.

Right now the vegetable garden was closed for the winter. Liberty was hoping they would grow her favorite vegetables. She liked baby carrots, zucchini, and corn best.

The photographer had Liberty put on her backpack and pose near the vegetable garden.

"Smile!" the photographer said. "Think of something funny."

"Liberty," her father called out. "Do you know what President Reagan's favorite vegetable was? Jelly beans! Get it? *Beans!*"

"Ha!" Liberty grinned.

"That was a nice and natural smile!" the photographer said. "Perfect!"

"Actually, President Reagan's favorite vegetable was radishes," Miss Crum pointed out.

Radishes? Um. That was unusual.

"Hey, Dad, I've got one for you," Liberty said. "What's President Obama's favorite vegetable?"

"Hmm," her dad said. "I heard he doesn't like beets, but I don't know his favorite."

"Barack-oli!" Liberty said. "Get it?"

"Good one!" her father said. "Did you know President George H. W. Bush hates broccoli because his mother made him eat it every single day? Aren't you glad you don't have to do that?"

Liberty liked broccoli with sprinkled cheese—but every single day? No, thank you! Bluh!

"Liberty, how about a smile instead of a yucky face?" The photographer laughed.

"Sorry!" Liberty apologized.

"Maybe that's enough veggie talk. Let's do a few

more shots in the Children's Garden and get that smile back," the photographer said.

The Children's Garden was Liberty's favorite! It was an area where some of the First Kids and First Grand-kids had their handprints and footprints in cement.

Liberty would get to put her print in when it got warmer outside. She had some plans for her prints. Every other kid had put either their hands or feet in it. Liberty was thinking about putting her elbows in it, or maybe her knees.

"Wheeee!" she heard from across the yard. Liberty turned to see James sliding down her slide. The best part of her new yard was the playground. And James seemed to think so too.

"Woo-hoo!" shouted James.

"Don't go too fast," Liberty heard Miss Crum say. "Be careful of your bottom!"

Ha, instead of her elbows and knees, maybe Liberty

would put her bottom print in the cement. Okay, not really. But the thought made Liberty laugh.

"Great smile!" the photographer said. "Very natural. You're done, kiddo."

Yes!

"And now, my turn to take my traditional picture," her father said.

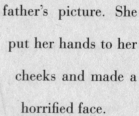

Liberty whistled for Franklin to come over to her.

"Say 'first day of school!'" her father said, as he always did. Liberty posed as she always did for her

father's picture. She put her hands to her cheeks and made a horrified face.

"Got it!" her dad said.

"May I play on the playset with James?" Liberty asked.

"You have four minutes and twelve seconds before you have to leave," Miss Crum told her.

"Then that would be three minutes and twelve seconds of yes," Liberty's mom said.

Yes! Liberty ran over to the playground.

"Watch this!" Liberty said. She hung upside down on the swinging bar and wrapped her feet over the top.

"Whoa," James said as Liberty flipped down.

She climbed up the rope ladder and dangled from the top. Then she climbed up to the little house and waved at her parents and SAM out the little window. Then she jumped on the regular swing and swung. She pumped higher and higher and—

"Watch me jump!" Liberty shouted. She prepared for takeoff and—

"Goodness gracious!" Miss Crum gasped.

Miss Crum's gasping interrupted Liberty's focus as she jumped off the swing. And this made Liberty veer a teeny bit off on her landing. She landed a little hard and fell forward.

Liberty heard gasps.

"I'm okay, I'm okay!" Liberty assured them. "No damage!"

"Liberty's hair! It's mussed!" Miss Crum shook her head.

Oops.

"Liberty's tights have a dirt spot! They might be stained!" Miss Crum said.

Oops times two.

"Could be worse," Liberty said. "It could be mud. President Kennedy's son fell into a fountain that was filled with mud. The First Lady tried to pull him out and got stuck too. A Secret Service agent used a rope to pull them out."

"That would be worse," her mother agreed.

"Liberty looks like a regular kid going off to school," Liberty's dad said firmly. "Just the way she should."

Phew.

"Hmph," Miss Crum hmphed. "Well, then. Mr. President, you have a meeting with the ambassador in four minutes."

The president came over and gave Liberty their secret handshake that ended in two bumps and a high five. Then a big hug.

"Good-bye, Mr. President," Liberty said. "Good-bye, First Dog. Wish me luck!"

Franklin barked a good-luck bark.

Liberty was finally ready to go.

"We will be there early, so that will give you a few minutes to settle in to your classroom before the rest of the students arrive," Liberty's mom told her as they walked to the car.

Actually, *cars* . . . which was a little crazy.

There would be a lineup of cars taking her to school! A police car would lead the way. Then some long black cars with dark windows. Liberty climbed into one of the big black cars. James climbed in beside her.

"Very weird," Liberty said to James. "It's so different from my last first day of school."

"Which part?" James asked. "Leaving from the White House? Taking a car and driver instead of a school bus? Having Secret Service agents stay in your school?"

"Yup," Liberty said. "Yup and yup."

Liberty's mom, SAM, and the other SAM got into the car. The car started driving away.

"I wish you were in my class," Liberty said to James. "Then I'd know somebody."

"You'll make lots of friends," Liberty's mom said.

"And SAM will be there, right?" James said.

"SAM, do you go everywhere with me?" Liberty said.

"I'll stay fairly close by," SAM answered.

Liberty had never had a Secret Service agent at her school. She wondered if he would have to sit at a desk. SAM was pretty huge. She didn't know if he would fit. He might have to sit on the floor.

"This will be great!" Liberty said out loud. "If I don't know the answers, SAM can help me!"

"Wrong!" her mother called back.

Rats.

"He can stand in the hot-lunch line for me so I don't have to?" Liberty tried.

"Wrong again," Liberty's mom repeated.

Rats.

"Can SAM at least carry my backpack around for me? This thing is seriously heavy," Liberty said.

"Wrong again," her mother said. "You'll carry your backpack, find your own answers, and be a regular, normal student. SAM will wait outside the classroom. You won't even know he's there."

Sigh. Well, it was worth a try.

Liberty looked out the window and watched the streets of Washington, D.C., whiz by. She still couldn't believe she lived in the capital of the United States. She hadn't been in Washington, D.C., very long, and she hadn't seen much of it yet. She had barely finished exploring her own house!

"It's a beautiful city, isn't it?" Liberty's mother said as she looked out the window, too. "D.C. was a planned city first designed by a man named Pierre L'enfant. He wanted a city with open parks and grand national monuments."

"Did you know Washington, D.C., wasn't even the first capital of the United States?" James said.

"Seriously?" Liberty asked. "What was?"

"Congress met in different cities, so they were each considered the capital," James said. "The capital was at times in Pennsylvania, Maryland, New Jersey, and

New York City. Then it finally became officially located in Washington, D.C."

"I didn't know the capital could move around like that," Liberty said. "Did they pick up the buildings and just move them?"

"No, honey," her mom said. "These buildings weren't built yet. They were built when D.C. was named the capital."

Oh. Hee. Right. Liberty grinned.

And then she stopped grinning. Because the car started to slow down in front of a building.

"We're here!" James said, sounding excited.

And that was when Liberty realized that before she could be a normal student, she had to be First Daughter Goes to School!

"Oh my," her mother said, looking out the window. "I thought if we came early we'd avoid the commotion."

There were photographers waiting out in front of the school. They were waving at the car.

Liberty looked at the crowd of photographers. The car windows were tinted dark so Liberty could see outside but people outside couldn't see in.

It was so funny she could see them but they couldn't see her. So she did her best cross-eye face. Then she smashed her face against the window so her nose was squished like a pig.

Oink. Liberty giggled. She cracked herself up.

"Liberty, do you know this isn't a one-way window?" SAM said. "They can see you."

Liberty jumped back in her seat.

Oh no! Liberty could see the headlines now.

FIRST DAUGHTER FIRST DAY OF SCHOOL HUMILIATION!

And a picture of her with her nose squished! You might be able to see up her nose! Everyone would see it. People from all over the world and even back at her old school would see her making the piggie face. People like Max Mellon.

"Oh no!" Liberty wailed. "Now everyone will call me Piggerty Porter, First Snorter!"

Everyone looked at her.

"I was making a pig face!" she explained.

"I was only teasing!" SAM grinned. "Nobody can see you. I promise."

"SAM!" Liberty said. "*You* messed with me?"

"Heh," SAM laughed. Then he put on his serious agent face again. "I thought a little humor would take pressure off you. Plus, I had a moment of weakness and couldn't resist."

"It was pretty funny," James said. "Plus a good lesson for you about behaving properly out in public."

Liberty crossed her eyes at him.

"Yeeps!" James said. "I'm sounding too much like my mother?"

"Good job, Whippet," Liberty said, using his unofficial but still excellent secret code name. "You remembered the Secret Signal."

Liberty thought it was important for all Secret Assistants to the president to be able to communicate secretly. Crossing her eyes meant James was sounding too much like his mother and not in a good way. Two winks meant *Meet me for a secret mission.* Pulling on her left ear and fake-sneezing loudly meant *Help, please get me away from Miss Crum.*

"I've been practicing in the mirror," James said proudly.

"Security is lining up," SAM suddenly announced. "One minute until we go in."

Liberty's tummy felt sick again.

"Liberty, are you ready to go to school?" the driver said. The car stopped.

Do not hurl. Do not hurl.

And then her mother turned around and smiled at her. Liberty felt a teeny bit better. And her mom handed back something that made Liberty feel a *whole* lot better.

It was a little keychain with a mini Jack Russell terrier squishy stuffed animal hanging on it.

"It looks like a teeny Franklin!" Liberty said, holding it up.

"You can attach it to your backpack," her mom said. "And when you get a little nervous, just remember it's always there for you."

"Aw," Liberty said. She attached the keychain onto her blue and white backpack. It looked perfect.

Liberty took a deep breath. It was time.

SAM opened the door and got out first. Then he held his hand out. Liberty took another deep breath, took SAM's hand, and slid out of the limousine.

Chapter 4

L IBERTY WAS HUSTLED UP THE SCHOOL
steps, surrounded by four Secret Service
agents, James, and her mother. She saw
photographers take some pictures of the group so she
smiled as she walked in the front door.

The principal was waiting at the entrance. Her name
was Principal Tingley. Liberty had met the principal
when her parents brought her to visit her new school.

"Welcome to your first day, Liberty," she smiled.

"Thank you," Liberty said.

The principal talked to Liberty's mom and SAM for a bit. Liberty wandered over to a wall of brightly drawn pictures marked FIRST-GRADE PROJECT.

"Aw, cute," Liberty said. "Pictures by first graders!"

If I Lived in the White House . . .

Oh! Hey! She was living that project.

"Hey," James said, coming over. "That's pretty funny. They did a project that's really your life."

My life?

"We do it every year," James said. "It's not about you, so don't get weirded out or anything."

Okay, that was good. And also cute! Liberty read what they wrote.

If I Lived in the White House . . .

- I would have a meeting for peace with all the world leaders.

- I would have a big-screen TV.

- I would be nice to all the guests.

- I would move my bed into the movie
  theater.

Hey. Now there was an idea! Or, moving my bed
into the chocolate shop. Mmmm . . .

- I would have my own pony.

Oh, yup. Yup and yup. Liberty so wanted her own
pony. President John Kennedy's daughter had a pony
named Macaroni at the White House. If Liberty had a
pony, she would name it Rigatoni.

"Liberty, it's time for me to say good-bye," her mom
said, coming over to stand beside her. Her mom gave a
little sniffle. "I'm so proud of you. You'll be a wonderful

student and classmate. Just like you're a wonderful First Daughter."

"Thanks, Mommy," Liberty said, hugging her mother. "Oh, and Mom?"

"Yes, sweetie?" her mom said.

"May I have a pony?"

"Sorry, but no." Her mother laughed.

Well, it was worth a try.

"Shall we show Liberty to her classroom?" Principal Tingley asked James. They all walked down the hall and around a corner.

"This is your classroom," the principal said with a smile. "And here is your teacher, Mr. Santo."

Liberty's teacher came out to greet her. He had brown hair and was very tall.

"Welcome, Liberty," he said. "We're happy to have you join us. Come inside when you're ready."

"Thank you," Liberty said.

"Good luck," James said. And then the principal and James walked away.

And Liberty was alone. Like any other normal, everyday student.

"I think you're supposed to go in now," SAM said.

Oh, yeah. Normal, everyday student except for the Secret Service agent.

"Aren't you coming in too?" Liberty asked.

"I'll be outside the classroom." SAM smiled. "Not inside."

Oh, right. Liberty went inside. It looked a lot like her classroom at her old school. Except in this one, the desks were pushed together in groups instead of in straight lines.

"Take a look around to see where everything is," Mr. Santo said. "The buses will arrive soon."

Liberty walked around the quiet classroom. She discovered:

- Her cubby. She'd be sharing it with someone named Preeta. Liberty hung up her coat but made sure not to hog the whole space. She shared her cubby last year with Perfect Paige. Perfect Paige had a big fluffy fake-fur pink coat that took over the whole locker.
- Her mailbox. Erp. Looked like she already had homework sheets in there.
- Her name on the class chore board. Today her job would be "Class Pets."

Class pets?

Liberty looked around to see what "class pets" might

be. She saw a cage on a table in the corner and ran over to it. Hamsters! Liberty loved cute little hamsters. One was fluffy and gray, one orange.

"I thought you might like to help feed Clementine and Stink on your first day," her teacher said. "Do you like hamsters?"

"Yes!" Liberty said. Definitely!

"Why don't you find your desk and unpack your things," Mr. Santo said.

Liberty noticed each desk had a name tag on it. She looked around at each group and . . . there it was! Written in bright green marker:

LIBERTY PORTER

She was going to be sitting next to a Preeta and across from a Jack and a Quinn. She wondered who they were. She wondered if they would want to be her friends.

Liberty sat in her chair and started to put her school supplies in her desk.

- Turquoise blue notebook
- A folder with a cute puppy with a huge head on it
- A folder with her favorite singer on it

- Freshly sharpened pencils

- Crayons and markers

- Scissors

- And pink, green, and yellow highlighters

Brrrrrspp! A loud noise made Liberty jump.

"And here they come!" Mr. Santo smiled.

Suddenly a bunch of kids rushed into the room. Kids tossing coats and backpacks into cubbies. Kids talking to friends. Kids running over to drop papers into a bin marked HOMEWORK.

Kids who were not noticing her.

Liberty sat up straight and tall. She put a welcoming smile on her face. She waited to be noticed.

La la la. Doo dee doo.

"Our desks have been moved around!" someone said. Then someone gasped.

"She's here!" the gasper said.

The whole room seemed to gasp. And stare at her.

"Hi," Liberty said.

"Yes, as I told you yesterday, our new classmate is here," Mr. Santo announced. "Everyone please take your seats and let's welcome Liberty."

The class slid into their seats, but nobody said anything. Well. This was awkward.

Liberty smiled a little bigger.

"Welcome, Liberty," Mr. Santo prompted.

"Welcome, Liberty," the class chorused.

A girl with straight black hair slid into the seat next to Liberty.

"Hello. I'm Preeta," the girl said. "Mr. Santo asked me to be your new student buddy. If you have any questions, you can ask me."

"Thanks," Liberty said. That made her feel good. Then a girl with brown hair slid into the seat across from her. She looked familiar.

"I know you! You were on the tour of the White House on Inauguration Day!" Liberty said.

"I'm Quinn!" the girl said. "That was so fun sliding down your bed and eating cookies! Our mom works at the White House. I mean, your house."

"Where's your brother?" Preeta asked her. "Is he late?"

Just then the door banged open and a boy raced through the door.

"I'm here!" he announced.

"Hey, that's Cheese Fries!" Liberty blurted out.

"I was hoping you wouldn't remember him," Quinn groaned.

How could Liberty forget someone who wrote "My name is Cheese Fries" on his name tag, asked her crazy questions, and started a beanie dog war in her room?

Cheese Fries looked around to figure out where his

seat was. He looked horrified as he stood in front of his seat and groaned.

"Is there a problem, Jack?" Mr. Santo asked.

Oh no. Liberty thought that he must be upset about sitting with her. She knew that some people might not like having the First Daughter in their class. She looked down at her desk and tried not to feel squirmy.

"I'm sitting with *three girls?*" Jack said. "And one of them is my twin sister?! Man!"

Mr. Santo raised an eyebrow and Jack slumped down in his seat. Liberty tried to cover up her smile.

"Mr. Santo! Mr. Santo! I'll switch!" a girl with red hair called out. Then she lowered her voice. "The First Daughter shouldn't have to sit next to *him*."

"Jack will survive," Mr. Santo said, and the girl looked disappointed. "Liberty, we usually ask new students to share something about themselves with the class. Would you like to share something?"

Liberty stood up.

"Hi, I'm Liberty Porter," she said. "And—"

"Eeeee!" someone squealed and everyone giggled. Liberty blushed.

"I just moved to Washington," she continued. "I live with my mom and dad and my pets."

"Oo! Ooo!" A girl raised her hand. "I know! You have a dog named Benjamin Franklin."

"And two sugar gliders!" someone called out.

Everyone was like, *Oh! So cute!*

"And you collect beanie dogs!" someone else said.

"People," Mr. Santo said with a laugh, "*Liberty* is supposed to be sharing."

"I think they know everything about me already," Liberty said. "Except—wait! I'm excited to be here."

Liberty sat down in her seat.

"We are happy to have you here as well," Mr. Santo

said. "And now let's take out our math books and read the beginning of page fifty-two."

Liberty tried to ignore a blond girl with a headband who was staring at her like crazy. Liberty pulled out her math book and tried to focus on that instead. She couldn't. Liberty finally waved back, and the girl looked like she was going to faint.

When Mr. Santo was on the other side of the room, Cheese Fries leaned toward her.

"Psst," Cheese Fries whispered. "Psst, Porter."

"Shush," Quinn hissed back.

"Porter," Cheese Fries persisted. "Are you buying hot lunch?"

Was she buying hot lunch? Why did he want to know that? Did everyone buy hot lunch here? Maybe Liberty should have checked before she packed her lunch. Moving to a new school was so confusing!

"No, I packed," Liberty said tentatively.

A big grin spread across Cheese Fries's face.

"Did you pack . . . cookies?" he asked. "Chocolate chip cookies?"

"Jack!" Quinn scolded him. "Sorry about him, Liberty. He's been obsessed with those cookies ever since we visited the White House. Even though he puked afterward."

"How many did you eat?" Preeta asked him.

"Nine," he said proudly. "Best. Cookies. Ever."

Liberty leaned over her desk toward him.

"Maybe," she whispered. "Just maybe I do have cookies in my lunch."

There. That would keep him being nice to her all morning, she bet. And, she *did* have two of those chocolate chip cookies in her lunch box. Maybe she could share.

Chapter 5

MATH MATH MATH.

Spelling spelling spelling.

The morning went good and bad. Spelling was good because Liberty spelled the bonus word right without even getting to study. Woo-hoo!

Math wasn't so good. Liberty didn't like math minute. She was only on level 4. And everyone else was on level 16 or something.

The best part of the morning was Class Chores Time. At least for Liberty. She got to feed the little hamsters their little brown pellets.

Things were quiet for most of the morning. Liberty was getting used to people staring at her. Most people seemed to be over totally staring, but a few people kept peeking. The teacher didn't call on Liberty once.

Mr. Santo announced a short break and then they would go to lunch.

"Finally!" Cheese Fries said. "Hey, Porter. Did you notice I didn't kick you under the desk once? I didn't ask you any rude questions? I didn't get you in trouble? Not even once."

"*I* noticed," his sister said. "I was impressed. I didn't know you had such self-control."

"I know!" he said proudly. "Every time I thought about it, I just told myself three magic words: chocolate chip cookies."

"Jack, Liberty doesn't have to give you her cookies," Quinn said. "Plus, maybe she doesn't even have chocolate chip cookies today. Maybe she has oatmeal cookies with raisins."

"Ew." Jack looked horrified.

Ew! Liberty agreed on that point.

"I do have chocolate chip," Liberty told him. "But I don't have enough for everyone."

"I'm the only person who can really annoy you all day, so I recommend giving one to me," Jack said.

"Maybe I should have tried to bring enough for everyone," Liberty worried.

"We only bring treats for everyone on our birth-days," Preeta said.

"You're not supposed to bring anything different from a regular student," Quinn said. "Mr. Santo has been reminding us to treat you like anyone else for weeks."

"Yeah!" Jack said. "That's why I can annoy you. Just like anyone else."

"Mr. Santo said that?" Liberty said.

"Oh yeah, we got the big lecture," Jack said. "'Just because she's the president's daughter doesn't mean you treat her any different from any other student. Blah blah blah.'"

"And we have to respect your privacy," Quinn said, nodding. "No taking pictures or things like that."

That felt weird. Liberty realized everyone had been talking about her before she got there. "Was anyone weird about me being here?" Liberty asked.

"Of course not," Quinn said. "Okay, maybe Sydney."

They turned to look at the headband girl. Her mouth dropped open and she knocked all her books on the floor.

"But she's harmless," Quinn said. "She was like that when she met the local weatherman. She'll get over it."

"I hope so," Liberty said. "I really do want everyone to treat me like anyone else."

"Cool," Jack said. "Then give me a cookie or I'll kick your desk all afternoon."

"Augh," Quinn moaned, putting her head down on the desk.

Then it was time to line up for the lunchroom. Liberty's place in line was behind Preeta and in front of a girl with wavy red hair.

Liberty felt a tap on her shoulder.

"Hi," the girl with red hair said. "I'm Harlow. I like your lunch box!"

Liberty did have a super-cute new lunch box. It had pink and brown polka dots.

"Thanks!" Liberty said. "I like your hair."

The girl smiled. They couldn't say anything else because they started marching quietly, single file down the hall. Just like her old school, the rule was no talking, hands to your sides.

Liberty turned a corner and noticed SAM was

★ ★ 75 ★ ★

standing nearby with his arms crossed. He turned around and winked at her.

When they got to the lunchroom, Liberty stopped after using the hand sanitizer. She wasn't sure where to go. And she saw people turn around and stare at her.

"Mr. Santo's class sits at the orange tables," Preeta told her. "I have to buy hot lunch, though."

"I'll show Liberty where to sit!" Harlow said. She took Liberty's arm and steered her to the end of one of the orange tables. She patted the seat on the bench next to her. Some other girls from Liberty's class were sitting there.

"That's Emerson and Kayden," Harlow said.

"Oh, my gosh," Kayden said. "It is epic that you're in our class."

"I know," Emerson said. "Like this morning, you were there by yourself in our classroom. I thought you'd be surrounded by bodyguards and nobody would be able to talk to you."

"Sillies," Harlow snorted. "She's a normal person like us. Right, Liberty?"

"Yup," Liberty agreed.

Then she looked up to see two girls standing and giggling.

"May we have your autograph, Liberty?" one of them said. The other just giggled.

"Um, I don't think we're supposed to do autographs in school," Liberty said.

"Do you have a sheet of homework or something with your name on it I can have, then, for my scrap-book?" the girl asked.

A lunch monitor came up to the girls.

"Girls, you'll need to sit at your table now," she said. The girls looked disappointed.

"Sorry!" Liberty called to them.

"You are *SO* not normal," Emerson said. "You're a celebrity."

"You'll get used to me," Liberty said. She started to unpack her lunch. She tried to ignore everyone leaning over to try to see what she brought.

"Hey, there's Preeta." Liberty waved to Preeta as she walked by with her hot lunch.

"Oh, she doesn't sit with us," Harlow said. "She sits somewhere over there."

Liberty felt a little bad, like she was blowing off Preeta. But she seemed fine sitting with Quinn and some other girls. Plus, this way, Liberty could meet different people.

Liberty opened her lunch box.

"What did you bring?" Emerson asked, peering over. "Let me guess. Sushi? Lobster?"

"No." Liberty laughed. "Of course not."

"Did your private chef make your lunch?" Kayden asked.

Actually, the answer to that was yes. But just for today. Liberty had asked if the White House chef could pack her lunch. Her mother said it was okay for a special occasion like the first day of school. But not each day. Today she had:

- A turkey sandwich just the way she liked it! (with nothing on it except turkey)
- Grapes (Red. Seedless, of course.)
- A cheese stick
- A silver reusable water bottle
- And two very large chocolate chip cookies

"I guess you packed it yourself," Harlow said, sounding disappointed. "It's just a normal lunch."

Liberty ate her normal lunch and answered questions about being the president's daughter.

"Do you get to ride around in that private jet anytime you want to?"

"What celebrities did you meet?"

"Do you get free clothes all the time?"

Liberty decided to move the subject away from herself.

"Do we have art or computers or something special today?" Liberty asked.

"Gym and wellness," Emerson said. "I bet you're really good at gym. You probably have personal trainers and coaches for everything."

Liberty shook her head. "I'm not that great at sports."

Liberty thought of her last gym class in her old school. They were doing a relay race. Liberty had run the wrong way and pretty much made her team lose.

Max Mellon had called her "Liberty Porter, Worst Sporter."

Nope. Liberty was not very good at gym. Hopefully tomorrow would be art class. She was good at art. And she couldn't run the wrong way.

"And tomorrow is music."

"I'm not so great at music," Liberty said. They had started musical instruments this year. Max Mellon had said, "Liberty Porter, Please Stop Playing Your Recorder."

"I'm sure you're great at everything," Kayden said.

"Isn't it so totally weird that everyone is staring at you?" Emerson asked.

"She's a ginormous celebrity," Harlow said to her. "She's used to it."

"It's different in your own school," Liberty admitted. She looked around and saw some girls gawking at her from a green table. They started giggling. Liberty waved to them and they all squealed.

"Ew," Harlow warned her. "Watch out. There's something behind you."

"Hello, ladies," the voice said. Liberty turned around to see Jack.

"Hi, Cheese Fries," Liberty said.

"You know Jack?" Harlow asked her.

"And I know what he's here for." Liberty smiled. She reached into her lunch box and handed him a cookie.

"Best. Cookies. Ever," Jack said.

"Now go away," Harlow said. "Boy-free zone."

"Gladly!" Jack said, and left with his cookie.

"Just what that boy needs, more sugar." Kayden shook her head.

"How did he know they're the best cookies ever?" Harlow asked.

"He was at my house on Inauguration Day," Liberty explained. "His sister was there too."

"They were at your house already?" Emerson asked. "You had people from our class over?"

Liberty explained how she invited the tour up to her room.

"Liberty, your room sounds really cool," Harlow said. "Maybe sometime we can see it. Hmm. We have a sleepover every Friday night."

Liberty saw Harlow exchange glances with the other girls.

"It's usually just the three of us," Emerson said.

"Everyone calls us the Three Musketeers," Harlow said. "But there's no reason we have to have just three of us."

"But isn't it the *Three* Musketeers?" Kayden looked confused.

"There's no law or anything," Harlow said to her. "We can be the Four Musketeers. Whatever. There *is* a rule you have to host a sleepover, though."

Ah. Liberty was starting to figure out some things about Harlow.

Suddenly a bell rang. Saved by the bell!

"Recess!" Emerson said. "Yay!"

Liberty jumped up and followed everyone as they tossed their trash away and went out a door to the playground.

"Hi, Liberty!" some people said to her along the way.

"Hi!" Liberty smiled and said hi to everyone.

"Hurry, Liberty." Harlow took her arm. "Come on!"

They went out on the playground. People were shooting basketballs, jumping rope, and climbing on the jungle gyms. And there was a really cool, twisty slide.

"Awesome slide," Liberty said.

"We practice over there," Harlow said, pointing to the grass.

"Harlow made up this dance," Kayden explained. "And we practice it at recess every day."

Liberty really wanted to go on the slide.

"Can we slide first?" Liberty asked.

"We don't have time to slide," Harlow said. "Recess is way short and we have to teach you the dance."

"And you can practice with us every recess and at our sleepovers and after school!" Emerson said.

"Uh," Liberty said. Liberty just did not feel like learning a dance right now. Or every day at recess . . . and at sleepovers . . . and after school.

And also? Liberty knew exactly why Harlow wanted her to be in her group. It was because Liberty was First Daughter! Harlow didn't even know Liberty and she wanted to be besties.

Liberty needed a rescue. Good thing she planned for something like this! Liberty raised her hands over her head and pretended to stretch. Then she waved the fingers on her hands.

It was her secret signal to SAM. *Come on, SAM! Ruffles needs you!* She did it again.

"What's the matter?" Emerson asked her.

"Just stretching," Liberty said. "Warming up for the dance."

"This is how it goes," Harlow said. "It's step back, turn left. Hop, jump, elbows, twirl. Then cartwheel!"

As the three girls danced, SAM seemed to appear magically by her side.

"Excuse me, girls. Liberty is needed," SAM said. He mumbled into his earpiece and looked very official. "Dbbbbr. Rbbbdubbr."

"Oh! You're Liberty's bodyguard, right? That's so cool," Harlow said.

"This is SAM," Liberty said. "Sorry, I have to go."

She followed SAM as he walked past groups of kids playing. Some people looked at her and whispered.

"Yay!" Liberty said. "My Secret Assistant Stretch Signal for SAM worked!"

"Now, I can't step in and rescue you every time," SAM said to her. "But it's your first day. And that girl seems to be rather persistent."

"Yeah," Liberty said. "She just wants to be best friends with a First Daughter. She doesn't even know me. And she wanted me to do a dance every recess. Every single recess!"

"Well, it is my job to protect you," SAM said. "And I was a little concerned when I saw the cartwheel move."

Liberty was not known for her cartwheels. She had several bruises and lumps to prove it.

"I just really wanted to slide," Liberty said.

"Why don't you join your friend on the slide?" SAM pointed.

James was walking around near the slide! Liberty hadn't seen James all day. She climbed up the steps and waited her turn.

"Aaah!" a girl screamed. "It's the First Daughter!"

Everyone backed off to let her go to the front of the line.

"That's okay," Liberty said. "I can wait until it's my turn." She thought she was doing a good job of representing First Daughterness. She wasn't bragging or cutting in line.

Then she zipped down the curvy slide. It was way faster than she had expected.

"Aaaack!" she screamed as she popped out of the tunnel and landed hard.

"Ha!" a boy said. "She landed hard."

"Liberty." James came running over. "Are you okay?"

"I'm good!" She jumped up. "That thing is fast. Want to play something else?"

"I'm fine," James said. "I usually pretend to be wizards with my friend, but he's sick today. And I think those girls want you."

Liberty peeked out of the side of her eyes. Harlow and the girls were waving at her.

"They want me to play with them every recess," Liberty said. "But I'm going to be friends with everyone! Well, anyone who wants to be friends with me. If anyone else does."

"I would say they do," James said.

Oh. Yes. There were some kids standing around sort of looking at her or trying not to look like they were looking at her.

"Do you guys play freeze tag at your school?" Liberty asked James.

"Sometimes," James said.

"You are so on," Liberty told him. "I accept your tag challenge."

"I wasn't challenging you," James said. "I'm not very fast at tag."

"I will crush you!" Liberty pumped her fist in the air. "I will take you down! You're going to lose with a capital *L*!"

"Oh no." James sighed. "This is where you tell me I have to show some spunk, isn't it?"

"Tag! You're it!" Liberty tagged James and ran. She ran over to a group of people staring at her.

"James is it!" she yelled. "Run before he tags you!"

People just looked at her. And then she saw Cheese Fries. She ran right up to him.

"James is it!" she yelled.

"It's tag!" Cheese Fries yelled. "Run for your lives!"

People started running around. James looked

confused for a second. Then he started chasing people. Liberty ran over to the playground. She ran up to Preeta and some people from her class.

"Freeze tag!" she yelled. "Run!"

There were a ton of people running around! James caught someone. They froze in mid-run! People were running! People were tagging! People were freezing! Then Cheese Fries was it!

Liberty ran and hid behind SAM, laughing. SAM stood very still with his arms crossed.

And then Cheese Fries ran up to SAM. And tapped him on the arm.

"Tag! You're it!" he yelled.

SAM didn't move for a minute. Then suddenly he started running with his arms out.

"SAM is it!" screamed Liberty, taking off. "Don't let him catch you!"

"Auh!" everyone screamed as SAM chased them.

Everyone was screaming! And laughing! As soon as everyone saw a Secret Service man chasing people, everyone wanted to play.

And then the bell rang. Recess was over.

People came up to SAM and high-fived him.

"That was fun," some people told Liberty.

"In my old school we played tag every recess," Liberty said happily. "But we never had a SAM!"

"That was exhausting," SAM said, wiping his brow. "That was almost as hard as my agent training."

Preeta ran up to Liberty.

"I wanted to tell you that when the bell rings, we line up by class," she said, out of breath. "Our class is this way."

Liberty lined up behind Preeta. She felt someone tap her on the back.

"You missed the whole dance!" It was Harlow. "But don't worry. We figured out your part."

Liberty tried to smile.

"Everyone follow your teacher!" a recess aide was yelling. The other lines followed their teachers into the building.

"Where's Mr. Santo?" Preeta asked.

"Where's our teacher?" everyone was murmuring.

Then the recess aide ran over and went right up to SAM.

"Please lead your class inside," she demanded.

"I'm—," SAM started to speak politely.

"You must be a substitute teacher." She sighed. "They always forget to tell you these things. Just take your class inside. *Now*."

SAM looked slightly confused. Then he went to the head of the line.

"Follow me," he announced.

"Your Secret Service agent is our line leader!" Cheese Fries cackled.

"This is so cool," Harlow said. "I bet we're the only school with a bodyguard as line leader."

"Class! Class! I'm here!" Mr. Santo came running out the door. He sounded out of breath. "I'm sorry I'm late!"

Liberty heard him apologize to SAM as they marched into class. Everyone put their coats away and sat down at their seats.

"Know why he was late?" Cheese Fries said to Liberty. "I heard him tell your agent that the other teachers in the teacher's lounge were bugging him about what it's like having you in class."

Okay, that was embarrassing.

"Everyone at lunch was bugging me about sitting with you. Like what do you talk about? Did you have secret spy pens and stuff," he continued.

Liberty decided she would keep a low profile. She would be the most normal person in class. Maybe even the most boring person in class, until everyone got used to her.

"Let's discuss how tomorrow will work," Mr. Santo said. "Everyone pull out your maps."

"What's tomorrow?" Liberty whispered to Preeta.

"Our field trip!" Preeta said. "Didn't anyone tell you about it?"

Field trip? No.

"We're going to the Smithsonian Museums," Quinn said.

The Smithsonian Museums! Liberty really wanted to see them. She had driven by them and looked at them. They were right down the street from where she lived. Her parents were planning to take her soon.

Maybe I can't go, Liberty thought. Maybe that's why she didn't know about it. It was probably too hard for her to go and bring SAM and the agents and everything. Liberty felt sad. Was being First

Daughter going to mean she'd be left out of fun things at school?

"Liberty," Mr. Santo called her name. "Come get your permission slip. Your parents agreed to have it signed in time for tomorrow."

Yay! She *was* going.

"Class," Mr. Santo said. "Let's share with Liberty what we have been learning about the Smithsonian."

"The Smithsonian is made up of seventeen museums," Preeta said.

"Where are they located?" Mr. Santo asked. "Quinn?"

"Most of them are on the National Mall," Quinn answered. "The National Mall is the big park here where a lot of the museums, monuments, memorials, and Capitol Building are."

"There are over one hundred and forty million objects in the Smithsonian collection," Harlow said.

One hundred and forty million! And Liberty thought her collection of thirty-seven beanie dogs was a lot!

"We are going to visit three of the most popular Smithsonian Museums tomorrow," Mr. Santo said, writing the names on the board:

- Air and Space Museum
- National Museum of American History
- National Museum of Natural History

Mr. Santo told them to circle the three museums on their maps. Then he told them to map the route they would take from school.

"This is going to be fun," Liberty said, drawing on her map.

"Ugh," Cheese Fries groaned. "It would be fun if . . . "

"If what?" Liberty asked.

"If he didn't have to be my buddy," Quinn said. "Our mom is making me be his buddy."

"That is going to ruin my field trip!" Cheese Fries said.

"Remember what happened the last field trip to the zoo when you were buddies with Lukas?" Quinn said.

"We didn't know that putting the seeds on Kayden's head would make the birds eat her hair." Cheese Fries snorted.

"Remember what happened on the field trip to the courthouse?" Quinn said.

"Ben and I were just playing tag," Cheese Fries protested. "I didn't mean to knock over that judge. Her robe was in the way."

"Well, Mom said you have to be my buddy," Quinn said. "And she's paying me five dollars to keep you out of trouble."

"It could be worse," Liberty said to Cheese Fries. "At my old school, this boy named Max Mellon had to be the *teacher's* buddy."

"That would be worse." Cheese Fries shuddered.

Liberty wondered who her buddy would be. She wondered if they had already picked buddies and she would be left over. Liberty never liked when teachers would make them pick partners. Someone always got left out.

And then—oh no! She might have to be the teacher's buddy!

"After you finish your maps, I have a sign-up sheet for buddies," Mr. S. announced. "Then team with another two so there are four of you in a buddy team to keep track of one another."

People were hurrying to finish their maps.

"Maybe our table could go as a group! Liberty could be Preeta's buddy," Quinn said, coloring her map.

"Oh, Liberty doesn't have to," Preeta said quickly. "Maybe her Secret Service agent needs to be her buddy. Or she might want someone else."

"Or Preeta can be buddies with a guy!" Jack suggested. "Like Lukas or Ben!"

"That's not going to happen," Quinn said. Jack sighed.

"I'd love to be your buddy," Liberty said to Preeta. She was relieved she had a partner. And Preeta was quiet but really nice.

People started running up to the sign-up sheet.

"I'm done with my map. I'll sign us up," Quinn said, getting out of her seat. She went up to the teacher's desk and got in line.

"Liberty!"

Liberty turned around to see Harlow standing behind her.

"I'll go sign us all up, okay?" she said. "You don't have to do a thing."

"Oh, thanks, but I already have a group," Liberty said.

"I made Emerson and Kayden be buddies so you and me can be together. They're groups of four? The Three Musketeers and you, our fourth musketeer!"

"Trouuuuble!" Cheese Fries said under his breath.

"Maybe next time," Liberty said. "Quinn already signed us up."

Liberty looked up to see Quinn signing the sheet. Then Quinn turned to walk back toward them.

"Oh, don't worry," Harlow said. "I'll talk to Mr. S. and get it straightened out."

She walked away before Liberty could say anything.

"It's okay," Preeta said. "You can go ahead and change."

"What?" Liberty said. "I said yes to you guys first."

"Ha, like that's going to stop Harlow," Cheese Fries said. "She wants the First Daughter in her group. And nobody will stop her!"

Liberty had kind of gotten that impression too. She sighed.

She watched out of the corner of her eye as Harlow talked to the teacher. Then she came back over to Liberty. She was frowning.

"Mr. Santo said no!" She looked shocked. "He said you were signed up for a group already and he couldn't change it!"

"Oh," Liberty said. "Yeah."

"Well, go talk to Mr. Santo," Harlow said. "Tell him you want to be in our group!"

"He already said no," Liberty said.

"Hello? You're the First Daughter," Harlow said. "He'll do what you tell him."

"I think I should probably let it go," Liberty said. Then she smiled. "But maybe we can all sit together at lunch on the field trip."

Harlow squinted her eyes and stomped off.

"Uh-oh," Quinn said. "Harlow isn't happy with you."

Okay. That was *so* not what she wanted to happen on her first day.

"You showed her," Cheese Fries said. "Liberty Porter said no way, José! Liberty Porter is *not* taking orders. Ha! That rhymed. Liberty Porter, you can take my order."

"Oh no, you sound like Max Mellon," Liberty groaned. "He used to say rhymes like that. Liberty Porter, First Snorter."

As soon as Liberty said that she realized she just made a mistake. A big mistake.

"First Snorter? That's dumb," Cheese Fries said. "I can do better than Max Mellonhead. Liberty Porter,

First Daughter. Liberty Porter, uh . . . First Snow-
boarder? No."

He thought for a moment, then grinned.

"Liberty Porter, First WARTer!"

Oh no. She'd created another Max Mellon. Liberty
dropped her head on her desk and groaned.

Chapter 6

THE LAST TIME LIBERTY HAD HAD A FIRST-day-of-school dinner, her mom had made chicken, baked potatoes, and green beans.

Tonight the White House chefs were cooking. They even put a menu on the table so everyone would know what dinner was going to be.

Liberty wasn't so sure about this dinner.

- Arugula and eggplant salad
- Lentil soup

- Green curry prawns

- Chickpeas

Yeah. She didn't even know what some of that stuff was.

The food was so fancy because it was a special dinner for honored guests. Her parents were hosting a dinner for some people from the White House cabinet.

"Cabinets?" Liberty had asked SAM. "*Cabinets* eat?"

She pictured a big piece of furniture opening its drawers and eating food. But then SAM explained that the president's cabinet was a group of people. That made way more sense.

The people in the cabinet were advisers like the vice president and the heads of departments like the Department of Justice or Health and Human Services or Transportation.

Liberty was seated between her mom and the

secretary of energy. The secretary of education was seated across from her.

"I bet I know why I'm sitting next to you," Liberty told the secretary of energy. "Miss Crum once told me I have enough energy to power your whole department."

The secretary of energy laughed.

"I tried to sit still," Liberty told her. "But there were so many 'My Father is Running for President' speeches. But look! I've been practicing."

Liberty pretended she was frozen solid. She smiled, sat straight, and looked straight ahead as salad was served.

"See?" Liberty said, barely making her mouth move. "I'm so still."

"Impressive," the secretary of energy said.

"She is really sitting next to you because she has granddaughters your age," Liberty's mom said with a smile. "And she told me she misses them."

"I bet I know why I'm sitting near Liberty," the secretary of education said. "It's because today was her first day of school."

"Yup!" Liberty said.

"How did it go?" the secretary of education asked.

"Good!" Liberty told him. "And not so good. Good was that some of the people were really nice. I got to feed the hamsters for class chores. My agent SAM played freeze tag and got to be line leader. And we're going on a field trip to the Smithsonian tomorrow!"

"Wow, those do sound like good things," the secretary of education said.

"The bad things were . . . people were staring at me," Liberty continued. "Then I was only on level four in math minute because I always freeze up when the teacher says 'Okay, you have *one minute.*'"

"That is tough." The secretary of energy nodded.

"*And* there was this boy who is trying to make me

crazy," Liberty said. "He called me Liberty Porter, First Warter!"

Liberty cracked up a little bit.

"Okay, that boy is actually kind of funny," she said. "And at least he treats me like I'm normal. Some other people wanted to be my friend right away because I'm the First Daughter."

"There are wonderful things about being the First Daughter," the secretary of education said. "And then there are challenging ones."

"Liberty does a wonderful job of handling the challenges," her mother said.

"I think she deserves some of the benefits, too" the secretary of energy said.

"After a hard day of work, I like to go home and relax," the secretary of education said. "And Liberty, lucky you! You live in a house with a movie theater. A movie sounds like a perfect way to relax. If I were you, I'd watch a wizard movie and eat popcorn."

Yes!

"And change out of dinner clothes and put on cozy pajamas and slippers," the secretary of energy added.

Yesssss!

"However, we certainly don't want Liberty staying up too late on a school night," the secretary of education said.

"True," Liberty's mom said. "She should probably be excused now before it gets too late. Change into your pj's and we'll ask the chief usher to help you set up a movie."

"Really?" Liberty said. "I don't want to be rude and leave dinner."

The secretaries of education and energy both went "Awww! Isn't she polite!"

"I did notice that you haven't touched your lentil soup or your green curry prawns," her mom said.

"Shall I ask the chef to make you a grilled cheese instead?"

Yes! Yes! And yes!

Liberty remembered her manners. She said a nice good-bye to all the cabinet people—especially the secretaries of energy and education. She even invited them to watch a movie in their pajamas with her.

They had to finish their dinner, though. Chickpeas were next. Too bad for them!

Chapter 7

LIBERTY RODE IN THE BLACK CAR ON THE way to school the next day.

But she was going to be allowed to take the bus on the field trip. The normal yellow school bus like any other student.

"Whoa, look at the police cars!" someone yelled as Liberty's car pulled up in front of the school.

"Look at all the big black cars!" someone else said.

Liberty guessed maybe she wasn't going to be exactly like any other student on the bus ride. She grabbed her backpack and got out of the car.

"Liberty, did you remember to pack your lunch?" a voice suddenly asked.

Oh yeah. Miss Crum had come to school with her today.

Liberty's parents had left that morning for a trip to Ohio. They were taking the president's private plane, Air Force One. That meant they could fly all the way to Ohio and still be back when Liberty got home from school.

"We have our field trip and you have yours," her dad had told her.

"A field trip is very exciting," Miss Crum said. "I will accompany Liberty to the bus. My schedule is light today since the president is out of town."

Liberty thought it was not necessary, but Miss Crum came anyway.

"Okay!" Liberty told Miss Crum, who was standing by the car with her. "I'm going to get on the bus!

You can go back to work now. Have a nice day!"

"Ah, I remember the days of riding the school bus," Miss Crum said. "I always wanted to ride in the very back seat. The cool kids said when you went over a bump, you bounced so high you would hit the ceiling."

"Hello." Mr. Santo came over to them. "I'm Mr. Santo, Liberty's teacher."

"I'm Chief of Staff Crum," Miss Crum said. "I hope you have a lovely field trip. This brings back such memories."

"Ah, did you go on a field trip to the Smithsonian?" Mr. Santo asked her.

"Alas, I did not. The memories this brings back are not happy ones." Miss Crum suddenly looked sad. "All of us children with perfect attendance were scheduled to go. I was so thrilled. And then I came down with the mumps and had to miss school."

That *was* sad, Liberty thought. But okay, bye now.

"I never got to go on a field trip." Miss Crum sighed. "And my cheeks puffed up like a chipmunk."

"That's a sad story," Mr. Santo said. "You should come with us. We could always use another chaperone." *What?*

Liberty needed a rescue. She did her secret signal to SAM. She raised her hands over her head and pretended to stretch. Then she waved the fingers on her hands.

Come on, SAM! Ruffles needs you!

SAM came closer. Liberty went to her next signal.

She pulled on her left ear and fake-sneezed loudly. She hoped SAM remembered what that symbol meant. It meant *Help, please get me away from Miss Crum.*

"Oh, my," Miss Crum said. "I hope Liberty isn't coming down with a cold. Perhaps chaperoning is a good idea, to keep an eye on her."

Oh no. Liberty stopped the fake-sneezing.

SAM patted his head three times and scratched the top of his nose.

Liberty groaned. That was the signal for *There's nothing I can do. Sorry.* Liberty was doomed.

"This is so exciting!" Miss Crum clapped her hands. "Isn't it, Liberty?"

"I think I need to find my buddy group," Liberty said.

She saw Preeta, Quinn, and Jack heading toward the line. She ran up to them.

"Hi, guys!" Liberty said.

"Hi, Liberty!" Quinn and Preeta said.

"It's Liberty Porter, Washington Explorer!" Jack said.

"Sorry about him," Quinn said with a sigh.

"What? That's a great one. I've got a bunch. I worked on them all last night." Jack grinned.

"Are you going to torture her all day?" Preeta asked.

"No," Jack said, "just some of the day."

"Begin boarding the bus!" Mr. Santo called out.

"Liberty Porter, Bus Boarder!" Jack hooted. "Two in a row!"

Liberty had an idea. She could give it right back to him!

"What's *your* last name?" she asked him.

"Our last name is Silver," Jack said. "And guess what? Nothing rhymes with Silver. NOTHING!"

"How did you plan that?" Liberty laughed.

"Three to a seat!" Mr. Santo called out, as the line moved forward.

"You, me, Preeta," Quinn whispered. "As far away from my brother as possible."

Liberty was almost to the front of the bus when Kayden ran up to her.

"Are you really riding the bus?" Kayden asked. "We thought you'd be in your limo or your private helicopter or something."

"I'm really riding the bus," Liberty told her.

"Harlow says to tell you that she's saving the backseat and you can sit with us," Kayden said. "And we made sure nobody else joined our group in case you still can."

Liberty looked up to see Harlow waving frantically from the back window.

"Tell her thanks," Liberty said. "I'm still in my group. But we can all sit together at lunch."

Liberty hoped that was a good enough answer, but she saw Kayden give Harlow the thumbs-down. And Harlow didn't look too happy about it.

So that wasn't a good enough answer. Liberty sighed.

She stepped onto the bus. She said hi to some kids from her class as she passed seats. She said a specially friendly hi to Sydney, the nervous girl with the headband. Sydney turned bright purple. She looked like she might faint. Obviously, she wasn't used to having the First Daughter in her class yet.

Liberty sat down next to Quinn and Preeta. But then Mr. Santo came up to her seat.

"Liberty, you're going to need to sit with SAM," Mr. Santo said. "That was one of the conditions of your riding the bus today."

"Oh no!" Quinn and Preeta both said.

Bummer. Liberty stood up and went ahead a few rows and found SAM sitting by the window. She slid in next to him.

"Sorry, Liberty," SAM said. "I have to follow the rules. The ride is only a few minutes. And at least we have this nice big seat to ourselves."

"Oh, *there* you are," Miss Crum said. And she slid into the seat next to Liberty.

"As I was saying," SAM repeated to her, "it's only a few minutes."

Liberty slumped back in the seat.

Another class filed onto the bus. A couple of kids

gasped when they walked past and saw Liberty sitting there.

"Hi!" Liberty said. She smiled at everyone.

"James!" Liberty said when she saw her friend. "Hi!"

"Hi, Liberty!" he said. "Hello, SAM. Hello . . . Miss Crum?"

He made a surprised face at Liberty. She shrugged. That wasn't a secret signal. That meant "shrug."

"Why, good morning, James," Miss Crum said. "Why don't you sit across from me. That way I can chaperone both of you. I'm sure your mother would like that."

She pointed at the seat across the aisle. There were two girls sitting there, giggling.

"Uh, I don't know these girls," James said. "So, I'll just go on back and—"

"Sit!" Miss Crum ordered him cheerfully.

James sat. Liberty could hear him apologizing to the girls.

"These seats are smaller than I remember," Miss Crum said. "And they are not very soft or comfortable, are they?"

She shifted around.

"I could use a little more room," she said. "Could you two please move in more?"

Liberty moved in. That meant SAM was squished up to the window.

"It's only a few minutes," Liberty whispered to him. "Remember?

"And what is that odor?" Miss Crum sniffed. "Do school buses always smell like socks?"

SAM sneezed. Liberty looked at him and he was pulling at his ear. Hah! Their secret signal about Miss Crum.

Liberty patted her head three times and scratched the top of her nose. Nothing she could do.

"Do you know how the Smithsonian was founded?" Miss Crum said. "A scientist named James Smithson willed his entire fortune to Washington, D.C., to set up a place for learning and knowledge."

Liberty didn't know that.

"What was interesting was that he lived in England and had never even been to the United States," Miss Crum added.

That *was* interesting.

"And his body is buried in the Smithsonian Castle," SAM spoke up. "Want to hear the story about how his ghost was supposed to be haunting the castle? When they dug up the body, his bones were mixed up. But when they put his skeleton together, the haunting is supposed to have stopped."

Miss Crum shuddered. "Quite distasteful," she said.

"Do you have any other stories?" Liberty asked SAM.

Miss Crum shuddered again and turned the other way. She stopped talking and began texting. SAM winked at Liberty.

"We're almost there," SAM said. "Look, we're passing the Air and Space Museum." He smiled. "That's the most visited museum in the world."

"We went there for last year's field trip!" James said, leaning over the aisle. "It was amazing."

He told her that they had seen:

- The Wright Brothers' original plane
- Charles Lindbergh's plane that he piloted for the first solo transatlantic flight from New York to Paris
- Amelia Earhart's plane that she piloted for the first transatlantic flight by a woman

"And don't forget the spacecraft," SAM said. "Like the command module from the *Apollo 11* that was the first to land on the moon."

"Liberty, there's a real moon rock!" James said. "It's more than three billion years old. And you can *touch* it."

"I totally want to go there," Liberty said.

"Schedule that on a day I'm working," SAM said. "I'll go anytime."

"We're almost there!" someone yelled.

"There's the National Museum of the American Indian," Miss Crum pointed out the window. "And the National Museum of African Art."

"Next year's field trip we get to go to the National Museum of Natural History," James said. "Dinosaur bones, models of animals, fossils of a saber-toothed cat and a wooly mammoth."

"And beautiful gems, like the Hope Diamond," Miss Crum said.

"I have to go there before next year!" Liberty said.

"It's awesome!" Someone's head popped up from over the seat in front of them.

It was Cheese Fries!

"Did you know that museum has a tarantula you can feed?" Cheese Fries told them. "His name is Big Bob!"

Ew! But cool!

"Young man, please face front and remain seated," Miss Crum said to him. "For safety purposes and because tarantula stories are quite distasteful."

"But there's more! There's hissing giant cockroaches that you can pet," Cheese Fries said.

Also *ew!* Also cool!

"Sit!" Miss Crum barked. Cheese Fries's head disappeared.

"I may not chaperone next year's field trip," Miss Crum grumbled.

"We're here!" James cried, pointing out the window.

Liberty looked out and saw a big building with a banner hanging on the front. It said: THE NATIONAL MUSEUM OF AMERICAN HISTORY.

The bus stopped and everyone cheered.

The field trip was about to begin!

Chapter 8

"T HE NATIONAL MUSEUM OF AMERICAN History is called the nation's attic," Mr. Santo said. "That's because it has such a random variety of items in its collection."

The class gathered around their teacher in the museum lobby.

Liberty stood next to her group, and SAM and Miss Crum.

"Buddy check!" the teacher called out suddenly.

Liberty and Preeta grabbed hands and raised them in the air. Quinn grabbed Jack's hand and raised it.

"*Ew*," he grumbled. "She touched me."

"Are you my buddy?" Miss Crum asked SAM.

"I don't think the chaperones need buddies," SAM replied seriously. Liberty tried not to laugh.

She followed her class into a dark room marked THE STAR SPANGLED BANNER.

Mr. Santo told them how a flag had been flying over a fort to show an American victory in the War of 1812. A man named Francis Scott Key saw the flag. He was inspired to write to a poem about it, and that poem became the national anthem. Liberty sang the song in her head.

Oh say does that star-spangled banner yet wave,

O'er the land of the free and the home of the brave!

Mr. Santo lead the class to a giant window and told them to look through it.

"That's the star-spangled banner?" Liberty gasped. The flag was ginormous!

"It's way bigger than you'd think," Preeta agreed. She read off the plaque. "It was thirty feet by forty-two feet but it was damaged in battle so it's smaller now. And the family that owned it gave pieces away as souvenirs."

The flag was still HUGE. Liberty figured it out in her head. It was more than six Libertys tall and eight Libertys wide!

"We have a lot to see," Mr. Santo said. "Let's move on."

They went downstairs to the lower level, where they saw all kinds of phones in the history of phones. They even saw Alexander Graham Bell's original phone. It was pretty much the first phone ever.

"All you could do was talk to someone on it," Kayden scoffed.

Liberty thought about her new cell phone and all of the games and texting she could do on it. Phones had seriously changed!

Then they went to a display on transportation. Liberty looked at all the old-fashioned trains and cars, like a Model T Ford from 1930.

"Sweet!" Cheese Fries said as he moved up close to see a motorcycle that daredevil Evel Knievel did stunts on.

"This is Jack's favorite room," Quinn explained, and then she raised her voice. "Jack! Do not even *think* about climbing in there."

Jack raced around the room, pretending to be driving the motorcycle. He bumped into a couple of people.

Liberty heard someone say, "Can you believe Liberty Porter is stuck in a group with *him* in it?" It was Harlow.

"I know, right? She totally could have been with us," Emerson said. "You asked her like three times."

"I think she's kind of stuck-up," Harlow said. "She only hangs out with people whose parents work in the White House."

What? That wasn't true. Quinn and Jack's dad did work at the White House, but that wasn't the reason she was in their group. Liberty wasn't stuck-up! She wanted to be friendly to *everyone.*

Maybe she needed to try harder.

She moved closer to Harlow, Emerson, and Sydney in the next exhibit. It looked like a big, old-fashioned kitchen.

"It's Julia Child's kitchen!" Miss Crum exclaimed. "She was my favorite chef."

"My mom makes the best chocolate cake from her cookbook!" Kayden said.

"I love chocolate cake!" Liberty said.

"You could just ask one of your private chefs to make it for you," Harlow said.

Okay, then. Liberty moved away from her for now. Plan A was: Try harder to be nice. Plan B: Try to ignore.

Mr. Santo said they were going to go upstairs to see the next room: ICONS OF AMERICAN POP CULTURE.

"I'm sure you'll recognize many items from modern times," Mr. Santo said.

"There's Kermit the Frog!" Preeta squealed. "And Oscar the Grouch!"

Yes! The famous puppets were on display.

"They don't have the coolest one, though," Cheese Fries said.

"I bet you like the Cookie Monster!" Liberty said. Cheese Fries gave her the thumbs-up.

People were running around checking out the cool displays. Indiana Jones's jacket and hat! Michael Jordan's basketball jersey! A baseball autographed by Babe Ruth!

"Come see my favorite exhibit!" Quinn urged Liberty. She grabbed her hand and pulled her over to a glass display. Inside was a pair of ruby red slippers.

The ruby red slippers?!

"I love *The Wizard of Oz*!" Liberty squealed. "I wore sparkly red shoes to preschool every day!"

"Me too!" Quinn said. "I wanted to be Dorothy so bad."

Liberty linked her arm with Quinn's. They started skipping around the room.

"We're off to see the Wizard!" they sang. "The Wonderful Wizard of Oz!"

"And you guys say *I'm* crazy." Cheese Fries shook his head. Then he yelped. "Hey! There's Muhammad Ali's boxing gloves!"

He started running around in circles pretending to box people.

"My gracious!" Miss Crum said. "Liberty, don't you think you should set a good example for everyone?"

That meant *Settle down, Liberty*. Liberty sighed and stopped skipping.

She walked calmly though the next exhibit called the Gold Room. It was about money. She learned that the first kinds of money included shells that were traded, and she saw different types of money used during the founding of America.

"Hey, presidents get their faces on money," Quinn said. "Maybe your dad will be on one."

"The Porter Quarter!" Cheese Fries said. "Liberty Porter, her dad's on the Quarter."

The Porter Quarter!

"Well, the quarter is taken by George Washington," Preeta pointed out. "I'm thinking it would be hard to change that."

"Yeah." Liberty laughed. "Nobody bumps George Washington."

The class walked through exhibits about wars, the Constitution, and musical instruments. There was so much to see!

Liberty learned how in the early 1900s one million African Americans went from the South and working in the fields, to the North and the cities in search of a better life. She learned about how millions of immigrants also came from Europe in the 1900s for a better life.

"Whoa," Preeta said, reading aloud. "They often lived ten to twenty people in one apartment with no electricity."

Liberty thought about the houses she had lived in. She was a lucky girl. Especially now that she lived in America's House: the White House.

"Next is my favorite exhibit," Miss Crum said.

They walked into a room called FIRST LADIES.

"The Gown Gallery," Miss Crum breathed. "The mannequins are dressed in the inauguration gowns worn by many First Ladies. Liberty, your mother's gown will be here as well."

Everyone ran over to look at the statues. First Lady Taft's floaty white dress. First Lady Johnson wore a bright yellow dress.

"Martha Washington's coat has pictures of *insects* on it," Quinn pointed out.

"I'm glad my mom's dress didn't have bugs." Liberty peered closer. She had loved her mom's inauguration ball gown. Liberty hadn't been so thrilled with some of her own dresses that she had had to wear that week, though. Especially the one that had a lot of itchy ruffles, just like her code name.

"Your mother's gown will go right over here," Miss Crum pointed to the end.

"I think your mom should pose like this." Cheese Fries demonstrated. He held his hands like he was doing a disco dance.

Liberty laughed.

"Or like this," she said. She pretended she was a chicken.

"Or like this!" Quinn posed like a muscleman.

They all laughed.

"It's kinda weird that there will be a statue of my mom in here," Liberty said.

"And your dad," Preeta pointed to the next room.

Liberty read the sign over the doorway: THE AMERICAN PRESIDENCY: A GLORIOUS BURDEN. It still didn't seem real that the words "American Presidency" meant her father right now.

"Class, what do you suppose 'glorious burden' means?" Mr. Santo asked.

"What's a burden?" Cheese Fries asked.

"A burden is a heavy load," Mr. Santo said. "Something that is done with difficulty."

"So it means that being president is a lot of glory but it's also really hard," Preeta offered.

Being president *was* a glorious burden, Liberty thought. She thought about that when she looked at the displays.

Abraham Lincoln's top hat was in the museum. Abraham Lincoln sure had a burden leading the country during the Civil War.

And there was the desk that Thomas Jefferson wrote part of the Declaration of Independence on. That was a glorious burden.

Liberty imagined him writing on that very desk.

We hold these truths to be self-evident, that all men are created equal . . .

"Wow," she said to herself.

"Look, Liberty's yawning," Liberty heard Harlow say. "She lives in a museum, so she's bored."

What? She wasn't yawning. She was *wow*ing! Liberty turned around to tell Harlow that she was wrong, but Cheese Fries jumped in front of her.

"Charge!" he yelled, charging at Liberty.

"Ack!" she cried. "What are you doing?"

"Did you see George Washington's battle sword?" Cheese Fries was pretending he was wielding it. *"En garde!"*

Liberty pretended to battle back as Cheese Fries pretended to jab at her. She battled as far away from Harlow as she could.

"Sorry," Quinn said. "My job is to control him. Jack! Control yourself."

"Aye aye, sir," Jack gave his sister a salute. "Check out that uniform." He pointed to George Washington's uniform on display.

"George Washington was really tall," Preeta said, looking up.

"George Washington was one of the tallest presidents. He was more than six feet," Liberty said. She had learned that from a research report she had written in her old school. It was called "The Presidents: Interesting and Weird Facts."

"The tallest president was Abraham Lincoln," Liberty said.

"Really?" Preeta asked. "Who was the shortest?"

"James Madison," Liberty said. "He was a foot shorter than Lincoln. Maybe you'd fit into his uniform."

Liberty had tried to put in some weird and interesting facts about her father. She had written that he burped after drinking too much soda. But her mother read the report first and took out all the good stuff.

Liberty moved on to another exhibit.

Now, here was something interesting and weird. She could have put it in her report!

It was George Washington's false teeth!

"That is so weird!" Liberty said. "Those wooden things were in George Washington's mouth. And now we're staring at them."

"I guess your dad's teeth could be in here someday," Harlow said. "Or maybe *your* teeth will be here."

"*Ew*," Liberty said. "I don't want my *teeth* in a museum."

"You might have to." Harlow shrugged. "You're the First Daughter. You better brush a lot."

Liberty shuddered.

All of a sudden a bunch of people started calling out from the other side of the room.

"Liberty! Come over here! You have to see this!"

Liberty ran over and saw a wall that had pictures of all of the presidents on it. And at the very end was a picture of her father: President Porter!

"My father's picture is in the Smithsonian!" Liberty gasped.

Pres-tastic!!!

She had barely time to think about that when people started calling again.

"Liberty! Come over here! You have to see *this*!"

She ran over to the *next* exhibit, ALL THE PRESIDENTS' CHILDREN.

The Presidents' children! Liberty's eyes widened. These were her people. She ran up to look at some of the displays.

There was a cute doll with a china head that belonged to the granddaughter of John Quincy Adams. Her name was Sally. There were games, a dollhouse, and some ballet slippers.

"I wonder if they'll put one of your toys in here," Quinn said.

"Maybe they'll put one of your beanie dogs," Harlow said as she came up behind her.

"I love my beanie dogs," Liberty said. "I mean, I know the museum is important, but I could never give one of them away!"

"Actually, they probably won't want just one,"

Harlow said. "They'll probably want all of them."

"All of them?" Liberty said. They wouldn't really, right?

"You'll probably have to give them up," Harlow said. "I mean, that doll was probably special to that First Daughter, but you have to sacrifice."

"Harlow! Stop being mean to Liberty." Quinn stepped in.

"I'm just saying." Harlow shrugged.

"You've been mean all day. Just because you're mad Liberty wouldn't be your partner." Quinn put her hands on her hips.

"And because Liberty is getting attention," Preeta spoke up too.

"Um—" Liberty quickly tried to think of something to stop all this. People were fighting about her?

That was the *opposite* of what was supposed to happen!

She had taken an oath of office. *I, Liberty Porter, promise to be an awesome First Daughter. I will represent the children of America, who are the future of our country.*

Okay, it wasn't a real, official one, but she'd meant it. Now, how could she represent the children of America if she couldn't even represent in her own class?!

"Harlow probably didn't *really* want to be her partner anyway," Emerson suddenly said. "She said Liberty is kind of a spaz for a First Daughter."

Quinn and Preeta gasped and looked at Liberty.

Liberty didn't know what to say. What was the perfect thing for a First Daughter to say? What should she say?

"I have to go to the bathroom!" Liberty squeaked.

That was the best she could do. She ran over to Mr. Santo.

"I have to um, *go*," she mumbled.

"I can have your chaperone, Miss Crum, take you," he said.

Oh no! Not Miss Crum now! She looked at Miss Crum, who was still happily gazing at the First Lady gowns. Liberty fake-sneezed and pulled at her ear.

"I can chaperone." SAM magically appeared by her side. "I'll return Liberty shortly."

And Liberty fled. She passed the First Children dollhouses and dolls and facts and pictures. She ran out the door.

"Bathroom?" SAM asked, following behind her.

"Well, I don't really have to *go* go. I just need to be alone and think," Liberty said.

"Let's go out to the car," SAM said.

"We took the school bus." Liberty sniffled.

"Well, there's also a car." SAM smiled. "Actually a lot of our cars followed the school bus."

That would work. Liberty followed him through

the museum. Her mind was racing. She sniffed. She felt like she was about to cry. She was feeling pressure. Perfect First Daughter pressure.

But how? Liberty felt the tears start to come.

Liberty heard James's voice calling. She looked up to see him waving to her from his class.

"Would you like to talk to James?" SAM asked her.

Yes. Yes, she would.

Liberty, SAM, and James went outside and got into one of the black cars. Liberty said hi to the agents in the front seat. Then she flopped back in her seat.

"Dbbbgr, Rugged," SAM said into his walkie-talkie and held it out to Liberty. "It's for you."

"Huh?" "Rugged" was her dad's secret code name. Liberty took the walkie-talkie and pressed the button down. "Hello?"

"Hello, this is the president of the United States speaking," said the voice that came out.

"Hi, Daddy," Liberty said. "Did SAM tell you I need advice?"

"I'm the all-knowing president," her father said. "Don't you think I just *knew*?"

"Really?" Liberty asked.

"No, SAM called me." He laughed.

"It's silly," Liberty said. "It's embarrassing. I'll figure it out."

"That's fine," he said. "However, there's a diplomat and a senator planning to get advice from me this afternoon. I could use some practice giving advice today."

"Okay, fine," Liberty said. "The problem is I'm not doing this right."

"Doing what right?" her dad asked.

"School! I'm supposed to be First Daughter, First-Rate Classmate!" Liberty wailed. "I'm supposed to be nice, friendly, and welcoming to all!"

"You weren't nice, friendly, or welcoming?" her father asked. "Were you mean and rude?"

"No," Liberty said. "It's just that people are already mad. They're mad I'm not their partner. They're mad I'm not in their group. They're arguing about me."

"Well, you know you can't expect everyone to like you," her dad said. "Even *I* didn't get one hundred percent of the vote."

"Not even close," Liberty agreed.

"Well, kind of close!" Her dad laughed. "Don't be so hard on yourself."

"Yeah, yeah, whatever," Liberty said.

"Ahem," her father said. "I'm the president. You're supposed to take me seriously."

"You're my father." Liberty sighed. "You have to say nice things about me. But they're saying I have to give up my beanie dog collection . . . and my teeth!"

"Your teeth?"

Liberty was about to explain when there was a noise. *Tap tap. Tap tap.* Someone was tapping on the car window.

"Rrrrrbbdr," SAM said into his earpiece. He opened the car door and someone slid into the seat next to her.

"I'm sorry, I'm sorry," Miss Crum said, panting. "I was swept away by the First Ladies' gowns. I neglected my chaperone duties! I'm usually so focused! I always have everything running smoothly!"

"What was that?" her father asked.

"Uh, Miss Crum is here," Liberty said to her father. Then she turned to Miss Crum. "It's okay. SAM had it covered. You can go back now."

"I'm a failed chaperone!" Miss Crum said, putting her head in her hands.

"Don't be so hard on yourself," Liberty told her.

"Excuse me!" she heard her father say through the walkie-talkie. "That's *my* advice for *you*."

"I've failed you!" Miss Crum said. "Let me make up for it! Let me at least help you now."

"My dad's helping," Liberty said, pointing to the walkie-talkie.

"Is the pressure getting to you?" Miss Crum continued. "The people who want to be your friend because you're First Daughter? And the people who want to put you down because you're the First Daughter?" Miss Crum asked.

Liberty was kind of stunned for a second.

"Wow, you're good," Liberty said.

"That's why your father hired me." Miss Crum nodded. "Put the president on speaker."

Sam hit the speaker button.

"Hello, Mr. President," Miss Crum said. "We need to help Liberty through these trying times. Coincidentally, we just visited an exhibit called *American Presidency: A Glorious Burden*."

"Really? Am I in it?" her father asked.

"That is not the issue now," Miss Crum said. "It also is a Glorious Burden being First Daughter. And starting a new school requires a delicate balance. However, Liberty has comported herself most effectively."

"Um," Liberty said. "I don't know what that last part means."

"It means you're doing a good job," Miss Crum told her. " A good job in a tough situation."

Really? Miss Crum thought so?

"Wow, Miss Crum does not hand out compliments lightly," her father said.

"But I'm not doing a good job," Liberty said. "I don't know what to say."

"You say what you truly think," Miss Crum said. "Except perhaps when it comes to those three girls who are envious of the attention you get. *Hmm.* On the other hand, don't say what you're truly thinking. That might get you into trouble."

Liberty thought she saw SAM smile.

"I've got it. Say what is in your heart," Miss Crum said. "What your heart tells you to say."

That sounded good. But . . .

"But what if I screw it up?" Liberty said.

"We will all make mistakes," Miss Crum said. "For example, I was too wrapped up in the First Lady gown display to be an alert chaperone. And right now, your father is making a mistake. He is two minutes late to a meeting with a senator. He is throwing off the schedule."

"Oh," her dad said. "Oops."

"Ruffles is doing her best," Miss Crum announced. "And your best, Liberty, will be good enough."

"Wow. Sweet!" Liberty said, meaning it.

"Thank you, Miss Crum, for that nice talk," her father said.

"Seems like I picked a good secret code name for you," Liberty told her.

"Sweet Lips!" Miss Crum said, happily.

Giving Miss Crum that code name had been an accident. But Miss Crum loved that nickname.

"Thank you, Sweet Lips," Liberty said. "Thanks, Daddy."

"I'd better go meet the senator," her father said. "Bye."

"If you need more time, Liberty, stay here," Miss Crum said. "I need to return to my chaperone duties. Lunch will be starting and I fear a food fight without my vigilance."

"I'm missing lunch?" Liberty said. That wasn't good. The White House chef hadn't packed her lunch today. Liberty had packed her own lunch. And it was special! It was one of those boxes with the lunch meat, crackers, and a little bag of juice. Liberty *never* got to eat those except on a field trip!

"I'm ready to go back!" Liberty said.

Liberty climbed out of the car. She took a deep breath and walked into the museum.

And then she heard a gasp.

"It's the First Daughter! Liberty Porter!" someone in the museum called out.

"We have you covered," SAM said. "You can keep your head down and keep walking."

No, wait. Liberty remembered what her dad had said. "Even just seeing a president is a very special moment for people. They'll remember it for the rest of their lives. Even if it's only just me."

Secret Agent Rottweiler was going to make somebody's day!

Liberty stopped and made herself smile.

"Hi!" She waved. "Hi, everyone!"

People were like, *Hi, Liberty! Hi, Liberty Porter!*

And then she heard someone say, "She's waving at me! Oh, my gosh!"

Liberty followed SAM to the exit door of the museum where the car was parked.

And then all of a sudden Liberty heard a lot of voices.

"Hi, Liberty! Hi, Liberty! Hi, Liberty!"

There was another group of kids in school uniforms standing in a group near the exit. Even the teacher was waving excitedly.

"Let's stop for a second," Liberty told SAM.

"I don't mean to disturb you," the teacher called out. "But our class watched the inauguration together last week. And we were so inspired when you started the chant."

Liberty remembered that moment. That moment she felt so proud and historical and patriotic that she had started chanting "U-S-A." And the whole crowd chanted along.

"Hey, Liberty! U-S-A!" a boy called out. "U-S-A!"

"U-S-A!" said another girl from the class. And a bunch of them started chanting "U-S-A! U-S-A!"

Now Liberty's smile was real.

"U-S-A!" she called back and grinned. And she pumped her fist in the air. "U-S-A!"

U-S-A! U-S-A!

The class marched on, single file. Liberty waved until they were gone.

Okay! That put her in a good mood! After that, Liberty was feeling much better as she walked up to the door of the lunchroom.

Secret Agent Rottweiler reporting for lunch, she thought. She put on a smile and walked inside. She got her lunch bag from the basket and looked around.

People were sitting at long tables and opening their lunches.

"There's Liberty!" someone whispered.

Everyone stared. Liberty smiled. Hello. Yes. It's me.

She took a deep breath and put her lunch down at a table with Harlow, Emerson, and Kayden.

"I promised I would sit with you guys at lunch, remember?" Liberty said.

Harlow smiled.

But then Liberty looked at the table next to her. She didn't know the people there.

"Hi!" she said. "Can we pull the tables together?"

They shrugged and said, "Sure, okay."

"What are you doing?" Harlow hissed.

"Being friendly," Liberty said. "If we move the tables together we can all sit together."

"But we don't want to sit with them," Harlow said. "That's why we're over here."

Liberty pretended not to hear her. She got up and dragged the long table next to hers. Everyone moved their chairs over.

Quinn, Preeta, Cheese Fries, and the rest of the class were at the table behind her.

"Hey, want to pull your table over?" Liberty said to them.

"Do you have cookies?" Cheese Fries asked.

"No," Liberty said.

"Liberty Porter, Cookie Hoarder?" Cheese Fries said.

"No." Liberty laughed. "I don't have any dessert at all."

"That stinks." He shook his head. "Your chefs should make you cookies every day."

"That's kind of what I want to talk to everyone about," Liberty said. She cleared her throat.

"Okay, everybody?" she said. Everyone looked at her. "Remember that room called *American Presidency: A Glorious Burden*? Well, that kind of describes First Daughters. It's so cool I get to ride in a limo and have a movie theater in my house and a president for a dad."

People were really looking at her now.

"That was the Glorious," Liberty continued. "But I also have the Burden part. Like, people staring at me. Practically all the time. Even when I bomb my math test or when I blow my nose. Or thinking I'm stuck-up when I don't know what to say."

"That would be hard," someone said.

"I just want to be normal," Liberty said.

"Gee," Harlow asked. "You sound too good to be true."

"She's the First Daughter!" Sydney burst out. "She's supposed to be perfect."

"Ha!" Liberty said. "NO! I'm not! I'm going to screw up. I'm really nervous to be new."

"You?" someone said. "You're nervous? But you campaigned all over the whole country."

"I know," Liberty said. "But you guys are in my

class. You might be my friends, if I don't screw it up! Plus, sometimes I was really embarrassing when I was out campaigning."

Cheese Fries laughed.

"Like when you yawned during your dad's speech?" he said. "And the TV person said 'Liberty Porter, her father has BORED her.'"

"You saw that?" Liberty turned bright red. "I thought they only showed that in one little town."

"Wow," Kayden said. "You're right. It's hard being you."

"Well, we won't make fun of you," Quinn announced. "You're in our school now."

Everyone was like, *Yeah!* Except one person!

"Okay, FINE!" Harlow suddenly stood up. "That was a perfect speech. She can be your president."

Everyone looked at her.

"President of what?" Liberty asked.

"President of the class," Harlow said.

"*You're* president of our class," Emerson said. "We had our class election a long time ago."

Then Liberty saw that Harlow seriously looked like she was going to cry!

"Did you think I was going to try to take away your class presidency?" Liberty asked.

"Well, you are the daughter of the real president," Harlow sniffled. "So you should be class president."

"I don't want to be class president," Liberty said. "I'd be terrible. I can't even find the water fountain by myself yet."

Harlow smiled a little bit.

"Besides, I'm too spazzy," Liberty said.

"Oh." Harlow frowned. "I'm sorry I said that about you."

Everyone went *Whoa!*

"No, really," Liberty said. "I *am* spazzy. I don't think it's an insult, exactly."

"Spazzy is fun," Cheese Fries suddenly said. "And don't you think the class president should be nice to everyone, though?"

Everyone said, *Yeah! True!*

Harlow sat down and turned red. She looked down at her lunch.

Suddenly Liberty knew exactly what to say next.

"I'm starving!" she said. "Let's eat lunch!"

And Liberty made little sandwiches out of the turkey, cheese, and crackers. And talked to different people as she ate her lunch.

Chapter 9

L IBERTY DID NOT SEE ANY MORE OF HER
family members in the rest of the museum.
She did see an early electric light bulb
from Thomas Edison and a telescope used by America's
first woman astronomer and a Revolutionary War
uniform and Clara Barton's ambulance.

And then Liberty's first field trip was over.

All the students walked with their buddies to the
door of the museum to wait for the bus.

Harlow yelled out from the back of the line. "We
call the backseat! Nobody take it!"

"Why does she always get to call the backseat?" Cheese Fries grumbled as he climbed onto the bus.

Liberty followed him on to the bus. She slid into a seat next to SAM and left room for Miss Crum.

But Miss Crum paused before she sat down.

"I always wanted to sit in the backseat of the bus," Miss Crum said. "I hear that you bounce higher over the bumps."

"Yes," Liberty said. "I remember you told me that."

"I think I'll find out," Miss Crum said.

And Miss Crum continued walking to the back of the bus. James came down the aisle and sat down in the seat across from Liberty and SAM.

"Where is Miss Crum going?" James asked SAM.

"It appears that she's going to the back of the bus," SAM said.

Liberty leaned into the aisle and looked.

Miss Crum was sitting in the backseat with a big smile on her face.

Then Harlow, Emerson, and Kayden all came down the aisle together. They headed to the backseat. Harlow said something to Miss Crum, and Miss Crum just smiled and patted the seat next to her.

"Please sit down so we can leave!" Mr. Santo called out.

Harlow, Emerson, and Kayden had to share a seat with Miss Crum! Hee hee!

"I think Miss Crum is on your side," James said.

Hmm. Interesting.

A girl came quickly down the aisle.

"Hi, Sydney!" Liberty said.

"Hi." Sydney stopped and froze. "Um. Hi. Uh. Liberty."

"Hey, do you want to sit with me?" Liberty asked. "I have room."

Sydney turned pink. But then she sat next to Liberty.

"Did you like the museum?" Liberty asked her.

"My favorite museum is the Natural History. I like the animals," Sydney said shyly.

"I haven't gotten to go there yet," Liberty said.

"You haven't?" Sydney asked her. "So wait. You haven't seen the sugar glider exhibit?"

"The what?!" Libery exclaimed. "The SUGAR GLIDER EXHIBIT?"

"Yes, there's a sugar glider display." Sydney nodded. "They're stuffed but they're cute."

"SAM!" Liberty said. "Is it too late to stop the bus and let me out at the other museum?"

"Yes, it is." SAM nodded.

"Nobody told me there was a sugar glider exhibit." Liberty shook her head. "SAM!" Liberty turned to him. "We have to go the Natural History Museum and see this."

"Well, everyone knows you live in a house that's a museum. Maybe everyone thinks you're an expert on museums," Sydney said. "It must be kind of neat living in a museum house. My mom signed us up for a tour of the White House so we could see it."

"Cool!" Liberty said. "When?"

"There's a waiting list of four months," Sydney said.

Four months? Her classmate had to wait four *months? Hmm. Hmmmmm.*

Liberty turned to SAM.

"All the parents will be at parent pickup," Liberty whispered to him. "What if they brought their kids over to my house?"

"Now?" SAM asked.

"I used to make last-minute playdates at my old school," Liberty said hopefully.

"You used to invite your whole class over after school?" SAM asked her.

"Um, no," Liberty said. "Maybe not the whole class. Okay, maybe one or two people. But I want to be welcoming! I can't leave anyone out, can I? My whole class. Oh, and James."

"Well, your parents did just get back. . . . " SAM said.

"Please?" Liberty said. "Remember my mission? Welcoming! Friendly! Not the snobby new kid! What could be better than inviting everyone over my house?"

SAM gave Liberty his phone.

The First Lady said yes, if it was okay with the chief usher. She called back to say the chief usher said yes, if it was okay with the First Lady. And if Miss Crum could chaperone until Liberty's parents got back.

And if it was okay with everyone's parents!

When the bus stopped Liberty made the announce-ment.

Everyone cheered!

"Playdate at the White House!" someone said.

"Let's go!" Cheese Fries announced. "To Liberty

Porter Head Quarters!"

Chapter 10

THE OFFICIAL WHITE HOUSE TOURS BEGIN in the Visitor Entrance. That's a hallway on the east side where everyone waits to get in to see the first floor only.

But not Liberty Porter's class!

Their tour began someplace tours don't get to go.

"It's the first time I'm bringing school friends home with me," Liberty said to her mom over the phone. "That's a special occasion, right?"

Liberty brought everyone straight to the best room in the house: the chocolate shop.

Everyone crowded around the White House pastry chef. Luckily, he was prepared.

"I made little White House candies today for the senators," he said.

He showed everyone how he took white chocolate out of tiny molds shaped like the White House. He said he could write anything on the chocolate in fancy letters.

"Cheese Fries?" Cheese Fries suggested. Everyone said that was a big *N-O*.

"Team Santo!" Liberty suggested. "That's our class!"

The chef wrote in beautiful cursive letters: "Team Santo."

He gave it to Sydney, who was standing next to him.

"I'll treasure it forever," Sydney said.

"No, you're supposed to eat it," the chef said. "You're my taste tester."

Sydney bit into it.

"Yum!"

"Now I'll make one for everyone in the class to take home as a souvenir," the chef said. "Or for dessert."

Everyone cheered!

"I dunno, Liberty," Preeta said. "This whole Glorious Burden thing? It seems pretty much all Glorious right now."

Yeah. Liberty had to agree with that.

"While the chef is making chocolates, we can move upstairs," Chief Usher Lee told them.

They all went upstairs. People *ooh*ed and *aah*ed over the big ceilings. The pretty artwork. And Franklin!

"He's so cute!" Emerson said, scritching Franklin's belly in exactly his favorite spot. Franklin had found a new friend!

Chief Usher Lee led them all to the East Room.

The East Room is the biggest room in the house. First Daughters Alice Roosevelt, Nellie Grant, and Lynda Byrd Johnson all had their weddings in it. There are shiny chandeliers hanging from the ceiling . . . and a particularly shiny clean floor.

Liberty knew exactly what to do next.

"Take off your shoes, everyone!" Liberty said. "We're going to SLIDE!"

Chief Usher turned on some music.

Liberty lined everyone up in three straight lines and led the way.

She took a running start. And . . . *woooosh!* Liberty slid down the hall. She was going at least four jillion miles an hour!

Everyone cheered!

And then everyone took turns sliding. Cheese Fries was first in line.

"Woo-hoo!" Cheese Fries hooted.

People were sliding around. Franklin was racing around, barking happily.

Chief Usher Lee brought out the sugar gliders in

their visitor cage. Everyone squealed as Roosevelt and Suzy took the treats they fed them.

"So cute!" everyone said.

Then Liberty noticed James standing off to the side with Miss Crum.

"Why are you standing with Miss Crum?" Liberty whispered to James. "You could have done the secret signal."

"I don't really know anyone in your class," he said.

"Hmmm," Liberty said. Then she saw Cheese Fries. He was sliding and crashing headfirst into the walls.

"I think I have someone to introduce you to," Liberty told James.

"Wise idea." Miss Crum nodded. "James can be a good influence on that boy."

"I was more thinking Cheese Fries could teach James how to slide that way," Liberty said. "But okay! Your idea too."

Liberty heard a cell phone ring from a corner of the room where the coats were piled up. She recognized the ringtone and got the phone.

Harlow, Emerson, and Kayden were practicing their cartwheels in one corner of the room.

"I think your phone is ringing," Liberty said, giving Harlow her phone.

"Hi, Mom," Harlow said. "Oh. Can't I skip dance class this one time? Can't I at least be late? I'm having fun."

Harlow listened and then hung up the phone.

"I'm going to have to go," she said sadly. "I have dance class every day after school. My mom says if I miss one I might screw up recital."

"Bummer," Liberty said.

"This was fun, though," Harlow said. "Thanks. I really am sorry for calling you spazzy. Before I go, want me to show you what you're doing wrong with your cartwheel?"

"Sure!" Liberty said.

Harlow showed her how to keep her arms straight and next to her ears.

Liberty tried it and . . . almost! Not exactly! But better!

"Sometime on the playground, if you're not playing tag or something, I can help you practice," Harlow offered.

"Thanks," Liberty told her.

Liberty waved good-bye as Harlow got her coat and followed Chief Usher out of the room.

"Yay! Now we can slide too," Kayden told Emerson.

"Hello, Liberty's classmates!" a voice said. "Plus James."

"THE PRESIDENT!" Everyone gasped.

Everyone except Liberty.

"Dad!" she said. She ran over to her dad and gave him a hug. And then her mom walked in!

"THE FIRST LADY!" everyone said.

"Welcome, Liberty's class!" her parents said to everyone.

Everyone was saying "Hi, Mr. President! Hello, First Lady! Thanks for having us!" Well, everyone except Sydney, who had to sit down on the floor because she was so starstruck.

"Do you mind if we crash the party?" her dad asked. "We bring treats."

And suddenly some staffers wheeled in a long table. And on that long table was . . .

"Ice-cream sundaes!" everyone yelled.

After that, the president and First Lady were forgotten while everyone rushed to make their own sundaes.

There was a choice of ice cream:

- Cookie dough
- Vanilla

- Swirl frozen yogurt

- Lactose-free chocolate ("Yay!" said James.)

And a choice of toppings:

- Hot fudge

- Whipped cream

- Strawberries

- Rainbow sprinkles

"Man," Cheese Fries said. "Chocolate chip cookies, sundaes. This is the life. You get to live like this every day!"

"No way," Liberty said. "Yesterday my dessert was raisins. This is a special occasion for sure."

"Okay, but you have an awesome room to play in every day," Quinn said. "Can we play freeze tag?"

"I have an idea!" the president said. Have you ever played freeze *dance*?"

Everyone except Liberty shook their heads no.

"It was my favorite in fourth grade! When the music starts, you dance, and when the music stops, you freeze. If I see you move, you're out!" the president said.

Okay!

A fast and dancey song went on! And everyone started dancing. James was doing the robot. Emerson and Kayden were doing their dance routine. Cheese Fries was doing the cha-cha slide. Miss Crum was doing . . . Liberty wasn't quite sure what she was doing.

Liberty did the bump with her mom. Then she disco-danced with Quinn.

And then the music stopped! Everyone froze. Liberty was frozen with her arm pointing in the air.

The president walked around and peered at everyone.

Suddenly Quinn's fingers moved.

"You! You're out!" the president pointed at Quinn. He called Kayden out. Then Annie. Olivia. Jawan. Out! Out! Out! They stood off to the side of the room and laughed.

Franklin ran around and barked at everyone.

"Franklin, you're out too," the president said. Then

Miss Crum was called out. And the music went back on. Liberty did the macarena with a bunch of people. Then she did the moonwalk and—

The music went off!

Uh-oh. Liberty was mid-moonwalk with one heel off the ground.

She tried to balance . . . tried to balance . . . and nope! She fell over!

"Liberty is OUT!" the President said.

Liberty ran off to the side and high-fived the other kids. Tejal was out. Nathan was out. And James was out. He ran over to where Liberty was standing.

"It was nice that you had everyone over," James said to Liberty.

"I was trying to think of a way to be welcoming, nice, and friendly to everyone," Liberty explained.

"You didn't need to invite everyone over to do that," James said. "You were like that in school. Like when you invited us all to play tag. And at lunch when you pushed the lunch tables together. And when you invited Sydney to sit next to you on the bus."

Really? Liberty thought about it. Maybe that was true!

Secret Agent Mission First Rate Classmate: ☺

A+

Awesome!

"Thanks, Whippet," Liberty said.

"Important announcement from the president of the United States!" Liberty's dad said loudly. "We're down to our three finalists! Who will be the winner of the First Official White House Freeze Dance?"

Sydney! Cheese Fries! And . . . the First Lady?

The music got super-loud. Everyone watched the three finalists! Who would win?

Sydney was dancing around with her arms in the air. Cheese Fries was doing the sprinkler. And Liberty's mother was holding her nose and doing the swim.

Go, First Lady!

Woo-hoo! People were cheering them all on. And the music stopped!

The President walked around and peered at everyone.

Cheese Fries was frozen with his arm out. Sydney had both hands in the air. The First Lady had her nose plugged and the other arm in the air. And then . . . Liberty's mom sneezed!

"The First Lady is OUT!" the president announced.

Cheese Fries wobbled. He was OUT! That meant . . .

"The winner is . . . Sydney!"

Sydney blushed. And then she bowed while everyone clapped for her.

"And now, everybody dance!" Liberty called out.

"An Executive Order from Liberty Porter!" Cheese Fries said. "Hey, that's a rhyme."

"No rhymes," Liberty said.

"You're lucky you have an awesome rhyming name," Cheese Fries said. "Liberty Porter, Total Disorder! Liberty Porter, Comes Up Shorter!"

"Um, those aren't exactly compliments," Liberty pointed out.

"You get Liberty Porter Supporter!" he said. "Liberty Porter, Time Transporter! Liberty Porter, First WARTer? All the good stuff!"

"Only my brother would think that 'wart' was good and not gross," Quinn groaned.

"Gross *is* good!" Cheese Fries said. "But okay, how about Liberty Porter is cool . . . sorta?"

"That was almost nice. Sorta," Liberty said. "A nice surprise . . . from Cheese Fries."

"Liberty, it's almost time for your friends' parents to arrive for pickup," Miss Crum pointed out.

"Okay! Last dance!" Liberty said. "Conga line!"

Liberty started a conga line around the State Dining Room! Everyone jumped in the line and step, step, step, kick! Her classmates! James! Her mom! SAM! Chief Usher Lee! Miss Crum! Franklin ran along beside them and barked. And bringing up the end of the line, the president of the United States!

And everyone—EVERYONE—was smiling!

"First Daughter Fantabulous!" said Liberty. "And . . . First Daughter Friendtastic!"

Many thanks to my:

CHIEF USHER: Fiona Simpson, chief editor

CHIEF *and* STAFF: Jon Anderson, Bethany Buck, Karin Paprocki, Alyson Heller, Bess Braswell, Venessa Williams, Paul Crichton, Katherine Devendorf, and Paige Pooler

SECRET SERVICE (LITERARY) AGENTS: Mel Berger, Lauren Heller Whitney, and Julie Colbert at William Morris Endeavor

FIRST HUSBAND: David DeVillers

FIRST DAUGHTER AND SON: Quinn and Jack DeVillers

FIRST DOG: Bradley Scruff DeVillers

LIBERTY PORTER, FIRST SUPPORTERS: Mark McVeigh, Jennifer Roy, Robin Rozines, Amy Rozines, Melissa Wiechmann, Alicia Inman, Lauren Arisco, and Lily Dipietra

Here's a sneak peek at
Liberty's newest adventure in

LIBERTY PORTER,
First Daughter
Cleared for Takeoff

IF YOUR FATHER HAS BEEN PRESIDENT OF THE United States of America for two whole months and you've been First Daughter *and* super-secret assistant to the president for the same amount of time, there are a few things you should know:

1. You get to go to cool places in your own neighborhood. Like museums that have dinosaurs, your mom's dress from Inauguration Day, and George Washington's false teeth.

2. You don't have to give your teeth to the museum, even if a bossy girl at school tries to make you think you do. (Whew!)

3. You have a great huge room to throw a party where even Chief of Staff Miss Crum will dance like a crazy person.

4. You don't get to have the White House staff clean up after your party. You have to clean up even the gajillion rainbow sprinkles that spilled.

5. Your Secret Service Agent will secretly help you sweep up the tricky sprinkles under the couch.

Liberty loved living in the White House. It was the house where every single president except for George Washington lived. A house where other First Kids had lived for more than two hundred years.

A house where more than one million tourists came through in a year! More than one million! Including kajillions of kids.

Liberty thought that would mean she would have kajillions of playdates. But that wasn't how it worked. She couldn't just walk down and invite people to come upstairs to her room and play.

She had tried that on her first day in the White House. She wasn't allowed to do that anymore. She had to make special plans for people to come over.

And she had no plans for today. That meant Liberty was lonely.

Liberty knew she was lucky she lived in the White

House. The White House had its own movie theater! Its own bowling alley! Its own playground!

But it would be nice to be able to share them with somebody today. Liberty had met some new friends at school, but today there was no school.

Liberty's teacher, Mr. Santo, had asked the class what they were going to do for the holiday weekend.

Some people were going to the ocean. Some were going to visit their grandparents. Someone was going camping. Everyone was going *somewhere*. Everyone except Liberty.

Then suddenly someone did come into her room. Franklin! Liberty's dog was back from his morning walk.

"Good boy," Liberty said, kneeling down to scritch Franklin behind the ears. "You came to play with me!"

Liberty picked up Franklin's favorite squeaky ball. She squeezed it in front of his nose and then tossed it.

Franklin looked at the ball. Then he yawned. Then he went over to his bed and circled it a few times. Then he plopped down on it and fell asleep.

"Wait, no," Liberty said. "Wake up and play! Look, your favorite tugging toy!"

Liberty waved his toy in front of his nose.

Franklin just lay there and snored.

Usually Franklin loved to play fetch. But apparently, all he wanted to do now was play dead.

"Franklin," Liberty tried again. "Wake up! You're not nocturnal like Roosevelt and Suzy."

Roosevelt and Suzy were her sugar gliders. They were only awake at night. So Liberty couldn't play with them now either.

Booooooooring. She needed ideas for something to do. Liberty looked at a poster on her wall. It was one of the posters her father used when he was running for president.

PORTER: A MAN WITH IDEAS FOR AMERICA!

Her father!

Maybe he would have ideas for his daughter.

Liberty took out her really cool turquoise cell phone.

She texted POTUS (DADDY).

That meant the president of the United States.

AM BORED. DO U HAVE IDEAS FOR ME?

Liberty waited. Then her cell phone *brrzp*ed back.

USE YOUR IMAGINATION.

That was the best he could do? Use her imagination?

Brrzp! Another text came in from him. Oh, maybe he had another idea.

CLEAN UR ROOM.

Liberty should change that sign of his.

PORTER: A MAN WITH IDEAS FOR AMERICA!
BUT **BAD** IDEAS FOR HIS DAUGHTER.

Liberty texted back:

I'LL USE MY IMAGINATION. KTHXBAI.

Okay. Imagination time. Liberty decided she would pretend she was on vacation. She looked in her dresser drawers. She pulled out a T-shirt that said FUN IN THE SUN and bright yellow sunglasses shaped like suns. She also pulled a hula skirt over her jeans and put on a lei her father got her in Hawaii.

Now she looked like she was on vacation.

Liberty took her extra pair of sunglasses out and placed them on Franklin's nose. Franklin kept snoring.

"We're on a relaxing vacation," she said. "Well, you're definitely relaxed."

Liberty then put a bath towel on the floor and lay down on it. She closed her eyes and pretended she was on the beach.

Ah, she could feel the pretend sun. The pretend

sand. Then Liberty pretended she was in the ocean. She plugged her nose and flapped her arms around like she was swimming.

"Liberty, I—" Liberty's mom had stuck her head into the room. "May I ask why you are rolling around on the floor while wearing a hula skirt?"

Liberty stopped flapping and sat up.

"I am on vacation," she explained. "I was using my imagination. It was Daddy's idea."

"Oh," her mother said. "Well, I hope you're having fun."

"No, it's boring." Liberty sighed. "But you're here now, so can you play with me?"

"Sweetie, I'd love to, but I have to go to a meeting downstairs," her mother said.

"It's a vacation day for the country," Liberty complained. "For everyone except you and Daddy."

"Honey, you know that the president and the First

Lady have many commitments," her mother said. "You're welcome to come with me. I'm discussing the economic and political realities of—"

Erg. No and no.

"I'll just be downstairs until I have to leave, then," her mother said. "Let your agent know if you need anything."

That's who Liberty could play with: SAM! SAM was Liberty's special Secret Service agent. He was very tall and had no hair. His shiny bald head made it extra fun to pat him on the head during duck, duck, goose. Yes, SAM was excellent at playing games! Now the vacation fun could begin!

Liberty grabbed a walkie-talkie off her desk. Yes! Liberty had her own walkie-talkie to talk to her Secret Service agents. She had decorated the walkie-talkie with silver nail polish and pink and purple sequins.

"Hello, SAM?" Liberty said into the walkie-talkie.

Zzzzrblt! Sppkt! The walkie-talkie made static noises, and then a voice spoke.

"Ruffles, do you need me?"

Ruffles? SAM never called her by her official code name. Liberty had thought up a way better one: Rottweiler.

"Um, who is this please?" Liberty said.

"This is Russ," the walkie-talkie spoke.

Oh. Russ. He was another Secret Service agent. But he didn't play hide-and-seek. He wouldn't let Liberty play secret spies with the walkie-talkies, and he never wanted to play zombie tag.

"Is SAM there?" Liberty asked politely.

"SAM has the vacation day off. Do you need anything?" Russ asked.

Liberty told him no thanks, and then groaned. AUGH! SAM was on vacation! Liberty pictured SAM

lying on the beach. She wondered if he wore his dark secret agent suit and an earpiece in his ear on the beach.

Liberty had only one last hope. There was someone else who might be upstairs in the White House. It was Abraham Lincoln. Well, his ghost, anyway. Some people thought Lincoln's ghost still haunted the Lincoln bedroom. Maybe today would be the day she could get his ghost to talk to her.

Liberty went down the hall. The Lincoln bedroom

was super-fancy. This was where Lincoln signed the Emancipation Proclamation. There was a huge bed in it, and Liberty pulled herself up on it.

"Excuse me!" Liberty called out. "Mr. President Abraham Lincoln? Are you there?"

She waited.

"I know you're shy," she said. "But I'm really bored and lonely. Everyone is on vacation."

Liberty waited a minute. She was about to give up. And that was when she heard it.

"Hello?" a low voice said.

Liberty almost fell off the bed.

"President Abraham Lincoln?" Liberty asked. "Is that really you?"

"Yesss," the voice said. "Yessss, it issss."

O H MY GOSH! OH MY GOSH! LIBERTY WAS
talking to the ghost of Abraham Lincoln!

"Hi, Mr. President!" she said. "I'm
Liberty! I live here now! But I sleep in a different bedroom. Yours is too spooky. No offense."

"Hello, Liberty," President Lincoln's ghost said.

"So this is really freaky," Liberty said. "Can I put
you on hold for a minute? I want to get my parents.
They'll never believe me."

"I can't stay long," President Lincoln's ghost said.

"I also can't hear you very well. Stand up on the bed and get closer."

She jumped on the bed and stood on her tiptoes.

"Can you hear me now?" she shouted at the ceiling.

"Yeeessss," President Lincoln's ghost said to her. "So you're bored because everyone is on vacation?"

"Yeah," Liberty nodded.

"I have been bored too. Maybe you can entertain me. Can you do the hula?"

Oh my gosh! Oh my gosh! President Lincoln could see her and wanted her to . . . what?

"Hula dance," he explained. "You're wearing a hula skirt and lei?"

"Oh, right." Liberty looked down at her outfit. She took a deep breath. Then she started to hula dance on the bed. She waved her hands in the air and jumped around the bed.

"I'm not the greatest dancer," Liberty apologized to President Lincoln's ghost.

"I can see that. I'm disappointed," President Lincoln's ghost said.

"Excuse me?" Liberty's jaw dropped.

"The first daughter should be a better dancer," he replied. "You're not Liberty Porter, First Daughter. You're Liberty Porter, Worst Dancer."

"Did you call me Liberty Porter, Worst Dancer?" Liberty gasped.

"Yes, I did, Piggerty Porter, First Snorter."

Wait a minute. Wait just one minute. There was only one person who called her Piggerty Porter, First Snorter. It was . . .

"Surprise!"

A boy burst through the door of the Lincoln bedroom. And yes, it was Max Mellon.

MAX MELLON! Max Mellon from her old hometown and her old school? Max Mellon who once told her she would probably sneeze green goo all over live television and he couldn't wait to see that?

Liberty's mouth dropped open in surprise.

"You look like you saw a ghost," Max said. "Oh wait, you just thought you were *talking* to a ghost. HA! I can't believe you fell for that."

Liberty sat down on the bed.

"What are you doing here, Max Mellon?" she asked.

Before Max could respond, their mothers entered the room.

"Hello, Liberty! It's lovely to see you," Max's mother said to her.

"Hello, Mrs. Mellon," Liberty said.

"We're flying out on vacation and our layover is here in Washington," Mrs. Mellon said. "I know my Maxie would love to spend more time with you, but we're happy we could sneak in an hour."

Whew! Liberty was worried he would be staying his whole vacation.

"Liberty, I'm sure you'll be a wonderful host and show Max around for a bit while I catch up with Mrs. Mellon," Liberty's mom said.

"Thank you, First Lady Mrs. Porter." Max smiled his best not-letting-grown-ups-see-how-evil-he-was smile.

The door closed. Max waited only one second.

"Liberty Porter Potty! Did you miss me?"

"No," Liberty told him.

"I wish I could have gotten a picture of you hula dancing like that," Max said, cracking up. "I could sell it to the magazines and make millions. Hula, hula!"

No more hula. Liberty took off her lei and slid off the hula skirt so she was in her normal T-shirt and jeans.

"Let's go!" Max said. "You have to tour me! Let's go see your room."

"Okay." Liberty sighed. They walked toward her room.

"I need to tell everyone what your room is like now," Max said. "Remember how your room used to be so messy? Now you have servants, though. So I guess your room is perfect. I can't make fun of that anymore."

Liberty stopped walking. She still had to clean her own room. That meant her room was messy. With a capital *M*. Liberty did not want Max to tell people that.

"You don't want to see my room. That's boring. You're in the White House," Liberty said. "You should see the *downstairs* part."

"Anyone can see that," Max complained. "I need the private-secret-behind-the-scenes places that only friends can see."

Liberty thought quickly.

"Max," she said. "*Downstairs* has a private choco-late shop."

Max stopped in his tracks.

"Chocolate shop?" he asked. "Like, eating *chocolate* chocolate shop?"

"Yes," Liberty said. "Yes and yes."

"Last one to the chocolate shop is a rotten egg," Max yelled.

He took off running down the hall. Liberty started after him but then stopped. She picked up her walkie-talkie and said something into it.

Life in the White House will never be the same!

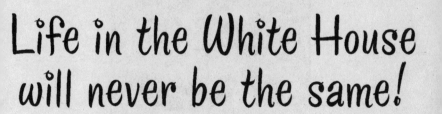

From **ALADDIN**
Published by Simon & Schuster

Enjoy this sweet treat
from Aladdin!